IN CALAMITY'S WAKE

In Calamity's Wake

A NOVEL

NATALEE CAPLE

BLOOMSBURY

NEW YORK · LONDON · NEW DELHI · SYDNEY

Published by Bloomsbury USA, New York

All papers used by Bloomsbury USA are natural, recyclable products made from wood
grown in well-managed forests. The manufacturing processes conform to the
environmental regulations of the country of origin.

LIBRARY OF CONGRESS CATALOGING-IN-PUBLICATION DATA HAS BEEN APPLIED FOR.

ISBN: 978-1-62040-185-9

First published in Canada by HarperCollins Publishers Ltd.
First U.S. edition published by Bloomsbury USA in 2013

1 3 5 7 9 10 8 6 4 2

Printed and bound in the U.S.A by Thomson-Shore Inc., Dexter, Michigan

For my children, Cassius and Imogen. For Jeremy.
And, with love, in memory of sweet Heather.

"Calamity is the perfect glass wherein we truly see and know ourselves."

—WILLIAM DAVENANT, PLAYWRIGHT AND STAGE MANAGER, FIRST TO BRING A FEMALE ACTOR TO THE ENGLISH STAGE

"The trail to the great mystic region
Is narrow and dim so they say
While the one that leads to perdition
Is posted and blazed all the way
Whose fault is it then that so many
Go astray on this wild range they fail
Who might have been rich and had plenty
Had they known of that dim narrow trail?"

—OLD WESTERN BALLAD FROM MONTANA

IN CALAMITY'S WAKE

Miette

‖‖‖‖‖‖‖‖‖‖‖‖‖‖‖‖‖‖‖‖‖‖‖‖‖‖‖‖‖‖‖‖‖‖‖‖‖‖

I CAME TO THE BADLANDS BECAUSE I WAS TOLD THAT my mother, a woman named Martha Canary, lived there. It was the man of God who acted all my life as my father who told me this. When it was time for him to die he made me promise that I would go and find her. I squeezed his hands and laid my cheek against his. His breaths and mine were staggered together, very, very weak for different reasons. I said yes because I don't cry and I loved him and in that last hour we were together I would have promised him anything.

You have to do it, he said. Promise me you will not change your mind. I know that you've heard sickening things and those things are all true but I'm sure she wants to know you.

I kept repeating my promise out loud, all the while hating the woman for not being the one who was dying. My father's brown eyelids closed. I stared at the window shades pulled down against the late evening sun and I felt amazed at how separate I was from him, how separate every person is from every other. And when at last I felt his long weak body release him, I sat in the dark with everything that was left, still promising, and fondled with my memory every detail of how he had loved me.

STILL EARLIER he had told me:

Don't ask her for anything. Just what was meant to be yours but she never gave you, and make her explain all the years she put you out of her mind.

I will, Father.

I let myself be pried away from his side and I watched from the doorway as the priest delivered last rites, drawing the glistening oil on my father's forehead. The drops of oil reminded me of the drops of water I had watched him draw on the foreheads of infants over all the years that were now being swept away.

I had no intention of keeping my promise. I did not want to meet her or even see her face. She meant less than ashes to me. But with my father's death, what happened and what was only an occurrence of feverfish, bright creatures of grief-fueled fantasy, all began to swim at the same speed. Each day after that, a little world grew in my imagination. The hours between my imagined birth and the moment I met my mother passed quickly as that world spun on its axis. Riding my horse, building my fire, saying grace over my food, sleeping on the ground, hunting, cooking, eating, always I thought of the man of God who took me for his daughter, and that is why I came to the Badlands.

Martha

||||||||||||||||||||||||||||||||||||||||||||||

CALAMITY WAS BORN FOR THE FIRST TIME IN Princeton, Missouri, on the first of May 1852. It was a leap year. This is the birth that she cited saying that the proof was in her flesh. Her name was Martha, no middle name or nickname to connect with her alias. Her parents were Robert and Charlotte of the hard-luck clan, poor farmers, poor in that they had no money and no talent and they found themselves on land that still dreamed itself as trackless forest.

Also born on this day, under the same stars, was Santiago Ramón y Cajal, Spanish neuroscientist, Nobel Laureate. The Taiping Rebellion continued. In France, Napoleon Bonaparte proclaimed a new constitution for the French Second Republic. Telegraphs replaced the semaphor. In London, the first public toilets for women opened. In the U.S., Franklin Pierce of New Hampshire, a Democrat, defeated a Whig. Nine men in New York founded Mount Sinai Hospital. A woman preacher wrote at her desk *Uncle Tom's Cabin.* On meeting her, Abraham Lincoln would later say, approvingly, So this is the little lady who wants to start a big war. Missouri was still a slave state and Dred Scott was respectfully suing for his freedom, dreaming night and day of holding an emancipation certificate in his hand.

In Mercer County, Princeton, the other living citizens were ordinary. Emma McRay slept in bed under rough blankets with two aunties and a cousin; her younger brothers snored on the bare boards of the floor. Luticia Nordyke fingered a stone cameo of her mother strung on a velvet choker as she nursed her fifth child, rocking in a straight chair, seeing nothing but the red light through her eyelids. Bill Lemons brushed his horses in the road so as to keep the stable clean. Margaret Hodson supped on potatoes discarded by the whores who lived in a big green house on Main Street. She felt vaguely ashamed that the whore who used to be a Puritan thought her a witch. People arrived and people escaped, always in the same mud-covered wagons pulled by oxen named for saints. Those big beasts bore the full load of so many homes and hopes.

SHE WAS said to be born for the second time in a common year. It was 1854 and she was named Jane Dalton at Fort Laramie in Wyoming. Her father was a trooper named John Dalton. Fort Laramie had been Fort John, a fur trading post, before it was taken over by the army. The fort was on the Oregon Trail, which extends 2,170 miles from its eastern departure points of St. Joseph, Westport, and Independence, Missouri, to its final destination in the Willamette Valley of Oregon. Oregon was the promised land of glorious climate and big-headed flowers, the Eden of dirt soft as water. The trail to Oregon followed the valleys of the Platte and North Platte rivers through Nebraska and Wyoming.

John Dalton policed the length of the trail, riding up and down the line of wagons, which were like a great segmented white worm rolling across the Plains. He felt the heated hopes of all those settlers pressing on his back.

The Brulé and the Oglala were camped four thousand deep. Pain in their stomachs grew loud as they waited on food promised by treaty. A wagon train of Mormons hurried to pass one last lame cow stumbling behind. The watching children were so hungry. Out of twelve hundred starving warriors stepped High Forehead. He killed the cow and fed his kin. The Mormons rushed to report this act as a theft, a breach of treaty.

Lieutenant Hugh Fleming sent word to Chief Conquering Bear that he must negotiate terms for the lost animal. Conquering Bear explained that food had not yet arrived for his people but, still, he would offer several of his best horses to the injured family. The horses were refused; hard cash of white-man money, twenty-five dollars, was demanded. The Mormons further insisted that High Forehead be surrendered to the army to be charged, tried and convicted of treason. Conquering Bear refused to give up the warrior for feeding the starving. The army was never supposed to manage conflicts like this—it was to be the Indian Agent, in this case the fellow who had yet to arrive with the promised supplies. And there was the problem of the translator, who was always drunk.

On August 19th, twenty-nine troopers (including John Dalton), the alcoholic interpreter, and Second Lieutenant John Lawrence Grattan ate breakfast and set out for the Brulé camp to capture High Forehead and bring him to justice. The troopers entered the camp yelling insults at the Indians, calling the warriors women. The interpreter vomited on the ground and raised his head to yell that the army was there to kill them all.

Conquering Bear signaled to his warriors to keep their arms down. We will not fight today, he said and then he turned away. Seeing the chief ignore his advance, Grattan realized that he would not get High Forehead. He ordered a retreat. One nervous trooper shot Conquering Bear in the back. The battle began.

Troops loaded cannons and fired into the camp. The translator wept on the ground. Soldiers scrambled behind rock walls and into divots in the stone. Red Cloud led his warriors through the mayhem and annihilated the thirty white men. Grattan lay on the ground coughing up and tasting his blood. He remembered a boyhood longing and looked fully into the sun for the first time as he died.

The Brulé men, women and children carried the heavy body of Conquering Bear as far from the camp as they could, away from white people and their money. They stayed, surrounding him, as he died on the Plains.

As retaliation for the loss of thirty white men, the army killed one hundred Lakota Sioux Brulé.

In the crisp bright fall of that year, Jane's mother was traveling by horse away from the fort when she was shot through the eye with an arrow. She laid her one-year-old daughter on the ground and removed the arrow with her own hand (what a sound it made). Blood and her eye fell on that child. For eight days she bled on Jane as she carried her. She traveled with the child in the darkness of night and they hid in the day. They ate weeds and roots. She arrived at Fort Laramie and gave over her daughter and died.

Sergeant Bassett and his quiet wife adopted Jane, calling her Calamity because of what had transpired around her pink, oblivious self. She lived in the garrison as the beloved pet of all the troopers, until she was fourteen.

THE THIRD story of her birth was an insult. She was the daughter of a madam who owned a whorehouse called the Birdcage. Her father was a wayward minister. In this way she was born three times, a farmer's child, a foundling, a bastard.

Miette

|||||||||||||||||||||||||||||||||||||||||||||

GOD WILL WELCOME HIM, THE PRIEST WHISPERED. All is forgiven.

My shoes became fascinating.

I saw a coyote carrying a man's skull down the road. Be careful to bury him deep or the animals will have him.

He's buried deep enough.

It seems horrible to think of one's bones being scattered about, but still, don't let the Indians hang him in a tree. It's not Christian. He liked these Indians, the priest mused. They seem to care for him. He wasn't a stray, though many are saying so. He was an Old Catholic, child. These wandering bishops, the way they make their own way away from the Church, I used to think they were all vagabonds but maybe he was right. Papal infallibility does seem less important here than the Eucharist. What could be more precious in this wilderness than bread and wine?

He looked at me for a minute. We have a name for what he felt for you, *aliena misericordia.* It means strange sympathy. It is what we used to say about men who took in orphan children. Now, I suppose we would see it differently.

Do you need anything else? I asked.

He performed services for the settlers, baptisms? Maybe he took confession?

He did.

He took money for this, I assume. Money for religious services.

No. He took food and clothing, some supplies; sometimes they helped us farm. Sometimes we helped them. There isn't any money, I lied.

He studied me. Because if there is money it should be given to the Church.

There isn't any money.

Will you live on here?

I don't know, but I won't offer services.

Well, I should go now.

Thank you.

BEHIND THE door I lay on the narrow bed breathing hard. I stared at the burial dirt on my hands, under my fingernails. I could still feel the weight of every spadeful singing in my muscles. The sound of friends working around me, throwing dirt on my father, moved in my brain the way no sound had ever sunk in and scoured about before. The walls and the ceiling were made liquid by my tears.

Aliena misericordia. It means stranger sympathy, not strange sympathy; he loved me even though I was a stranger. He was never insulted to be called a wandering bishop. He was an *episcopus vagans.* A man of God consecrated by God, living outside the structures and canons of the Church. He was his own vision of God's work, better, clearer, more humane. Not interested in selling faith.

He taught me that myths are neither true nor fair. Slaves

were not servile by nature but beaten into submission. The Indians, he said, were never savages but perhaps the Europeans were. Indians do not particularly stand for nature and neither do women. A woman's brain, he said, is smaller than a man's because her skull is smaller. A woman's mind is a different thing that has no natural limits. Children are not immoral at birth but new and possessed of great potential. The poor are not weak or debauched but just poor. The rich are not wise or deserved but just rich. People of every race and nation love their children equally and if it does not always seem that way it is because we do not love the children of others well enough. Christians are not in possession of a unique appendage in the soul. Priests are not better or kinder or more moral on average than farmers. Wolves do not embody Satan or devilry at all. The world is precious and it is a gift, but we are not the recipients. To think that we are the masters or owners is to imagine we could be excised from the world with no trace of us left. I muttered to myself the things that he had told me and remembered him a thousand ways, lecturing me in the evenings when I was wakeful, walking beside me, sitting in a chair reading, making me eggs, standing at the stove beside me while the hen scratched under the kitchen table.

I lay in my narrow bed thinking, this is the evening of his last earthly day. The long harmonizing of faraway wolves drifted into the room. I breathed grief in and blew it out again.

I remembered him explaining himself, kneading bread, leaning the red heels of his palms into the dough as if it could be sculpted to hold ideas. I remembered watching him and all my fears of life or death, of darkness, illness or abandonment dissolving.

Father, I—

The Old Church believes in unity in diversity, he said. In the old theology, Church meant reconciliation. Taste this, he said.

I looked down from his face, the length of his arm, at the green leaf pinched between the fingers of his hand, which was crusted with flour. I smelled the bruised herb.

Reconciliation?

God never meant, he told me gently, for us to devalue Earth to dignify Heaven. God never meant for eternity to devalue the present.

Father, I—

Go find her.

Martha

|||||||||||||||||||||||||||||||||||||||||||||

S HE LOVED CACTUS HONEY, COULD DRINK A JAR DRY.
She was six foot when hardly anyone was tall. Her face was
long and wide; she had a lantern jaw. Her eyes were small and
narrow but so light-colored that they glowed over her cheekbones. Even as a girl (*grr-ill*, she always said) she was too strong,
too square, too solid in her back and legs to be pretty. She was
three before she walked and five before she spoke. Like every
child she sketched pictures of her family. She fought with her
siblings and sulked when she lost. She imagined herself grown
up and the ranch she would have and all the horses she would
ride. She was built to ride horses. Her knees turned out
slightly, her tailbone lacked the usual nerves, and her thighs
were large and strong. Her hair was always dirty but it was the
same dust brown when it was clean. Her skin tanned dark as
milk chocolate in the summer and never lightened much
even when the snow was to her knees. Her mouth, which in
pictures is thin and ungenerous, was often broadly cheery
and quick to laugh. She had scars up and down her back and
the backs of her legs from a first, unsuccessful romance. She
stank of whisky, urine and sweat, but so did all her heroes.
She kissed the warm muzzle of her horse several times a day
and rubbed her forehead on the velvet there and whispered

love-talk. She slept outside on the ground to let the moon-light wash out her dry eyes. If it rained she rolled under a wagon and watched the dirt get spanked. The middle finger of her left hand was twisted from breaking under the stomp of a pony she shoed when she was nine. She begged her father on her knees not to beat that pony. Her voice was lighter and sweeter than you would expect, although it's true she knew fifty words for penis. But she also knew a dozen old-time songs that she crooned over the fevered heads of humans. She dug the graves herself for those that didn't make it and often she cried over them alone. Only once, she ate an orange. It was a gift from a Chinaman she rescued from a bear. She said the taste was Heaven.

You'll never read all that in a census. You'll never get to see her under the dirt, a little girl square-dancing, dodging corncobs thrown at her by husky boys. You won't find her human moments on any reels of film, or on a postcard. What you can see of her are only poses, subject to the decaying effect of legend. She had a favorite gun given to her by Buffalo Bill but she sold it in an act of drunken desperation. She had a favorite buckskin suit made for her by loyal friends so that she could perform onstage. It was beaded and fringed and it came with shiny high leather boots. She lost it all somehow. But know this: when she was asked for help the only word she knew was yes.

Miette

||||||||||||||||||||||||||||||||||||||||||||

M RS. NIXON RODE UP THE DUSTY PATH TO WHERE I
stood, brushing out my horse. She slipped down, holding her skirts to cover her legs, and untied a pack. She raised
her eyebrows, looking me over.

Are those your father's clothes?

I followed her gaze down my body and saw the oversized
gray work shirt tucked in with a tightly cinched belt (I had
punched a new hole halfway down and the tongue of the belt
lolled against my hip), the rolled-up bottoms of my trousers
and the dust on the man's boots.

Yes, I said. I thought it would be better for riding.

You're right, she said. My husband sent me to stop you. I
brought you some food, bread and canned goods, for your
journey.

Thank you.

She put the pack down on the ground. Stay in a house
whenever you can, she said. Your father meant well but no
doubt he did not understand the specific dangers of being a
woman. Your father was a good man. He helped us so much.
You both did.

I know.

He was a good, good man. She patted my horse's neck.

NATALEE CAPLE

I know. Thank you for these, I said, lifting the pack.

Mrs. Nixon wiped her eyes with the back of her hand.

My father died when I was eight, she said. She looked up at the bright curved sky. I felt so cold. Like the sun was gone. You be careful. Sleep in houses, like I said. Turn around and come back if it gets too hard. We'll keep watch on the house and your things. I guess you will be back in a few months. Send a wire if you won't. I hate to say goodbye. It's my least favorite word. Oh hush, she chided herself. Hush, hush, hush.

She put her arms around my horse's neck and let tears roll into her mane.

Are you all right?

Yes, yes. I'm fine. I'm just a silly, emotional woman. It's just that most often when people leave they never do come back.

She let go of my horse and wiped her cheeks with her hands and dried her hands in her skirts.

It takes so much to go somewhere else. No one really calculates what it will take to come back. Well, she said, don't ride at night. Sleep away from the road if you can't sleep in a house. I brought you this. She reached into a pocket hidden in the folds of her dress and drew out a Derringer and pressed it into my hand. I know it looks demure but one like it was bold enough to kill Lincoln.

I have a rifle.

I know you do and that's good for hunting but a lady alone should always have a little gun under her pillow.

You're very kind, I said, turning the metal comma in my hand, examining the decorative scrolls on the metal handle.

Look, you need to know how to hold it. Give it to me.

I handed her the gun.

There are two ways to hold this. Like this, she said, pointing the gun at me. And like this, she said, pointing the muzzle to her forehead, between her eyes. One likes to believe in the goodness of people. But the people you meet on the road, well, sometimes the unseen cannot really see themselves.

I'll be careful.

She reached out a hand and tucked a loose strand of hair behind my ear. I could cut your hair, she said softly. It would grow back, but at least from a distance you might be taken for a boy.

I'll be all right.

I'll pray for you. Don't pick up every stray you meet.

I won't.

You will, but I'll pray for you.

Martha

‖‖‖‖‖‖‖‖‖‖‖‖‖‖‖‖‖‖‖‖‖‖‖‖‖‖‖‖‖‖‖‖‖‖‖‖

S HE LOVED TO RIDE IN THE EARLY EVENING AND eavesdrop on the birds' last interrogations. The coyotes yipped to each other as they skimmed between trees. Sometimes the timber wolves would sing and the long notes drifted down from the hills, causing grazing deer to scatter. This was her world, emerging with each pointed star. She was eleven and nothing had been lost.

They lived in a drafty shack their father had erected by the river in Jackson County. It was three miles to town and often at night she rode to get her father from the saloon. On one of these nights she missed him as he headed home on foot or else slipped down the street to visit a woman. The manager knew her well. He was a kind man who packaged up the kitchen scraps for her to take home. This night, while he was scraping plates and cutting boards for her, militiamen appeared.

They came in through the saloon doors toting rifles, which they pointed at the ceiling. They were a ragged bunch in uniforms assembled from the odds and ends of many wardrobes, dusty pants of black, navy and green, shirts that gaped where buttons had been broken. Their jackets, shades of blue, were ornamented with handmade medals and patches embroidered with the Union flag. If it were not for the color of their jackets and the flags they could as easily have been Southern Guerrillas or road agents. Martha recognized two as brothers who worked on a cattle farm nearby. The group was unified by bandoliers full of bullets wrapped around their waists and chests. There were twenty-five of them in rows. The captain and two guards were at the front, then six and six and five and five. The bartender greeted them politely, polishing a glass until it disappeared. Martha fell back against a wall and slipped down, squatting in a corner. The manager came out to speak to the captain. He shook hands helplessly as he listened to demands. The captain nodded and with that permission the remaining customers slipped past the soldiers out the door.

Martha began creeping heel to toe towards the foot of the staircase. She managed three steps before a guard ordered her to stop.

She's just a kid, looking for her father, the manager said.

We're hungry, said the captain flatly.

I'll feed you. I'm happy to feed you, said the manager.

An anxious banquet began with the men seated, uneasy, stomachs growling, as the manager rushed to stuff bits of rag beneath uneven table legs. A big hand smacked the top of his head as he kneeled. Deep voices joined in laughter. The bartender rushed the drinks, cursing when they splashed. The men drank without speaking. Glasses banged down on tables were whisked away. Cigarette smoke clouded Martha's view. At times the smoke seemed to come from nowhere and at times it seemed as if everyone was smoking.

Finally, giant platters of meat and vats of mashed potato and buckets of gravy and colanders full of vegetables (for they must have run out of platters and vats) were carried into the hall by children. In an effort to soften the mood the town had sent the youngest citizens to the saloon to make their little lives more visible. The doctor's daughter in her plainest dress carried the gravy, *ow*-ing every time it splashed. The blacksmith's son carried carrots. The main street store's little broom-boy brought in the mash. The youngest whore in the brothel bore the meat.

The men ate without removing their hats. Darkly digestive sounds traveled around the room. Martha, hidden in a corner, watched the bartender watch the men.

When everything was devoured the children swept the tables clean and exited through the kitchen out the back door. The women entered.

There were three with hair piled in swirls over black feathers. Purple, gold, red and black ribbons weighted with beads on the ends ran from underneath bright wigs to the floor. The women twisted hips and shoulders tensely one way and then the other. Paste jewels on fingers and earlobes refracted green and white under the flickering lamplight.

They danced towards the men, distributing tin crowns to sweaty heads, anointing each scalp with a kiss. It seemed at last as if a real party had broken out when the rifles were placed against the walls and the men allowed their collars to be twisted and their cheeks to be pinched by the three dancing sirens. One man pushed his hand down the front of a dancer's dress and squeezed her breast, dragging it out of her bodice and twisting the nipple until she shrieked and smacked at his shoulders begging to be let go. The captain barked and the three women retreated in tears to the kitchen.

Gentlemen, shouted the manager anxiously, haven't we

fed you well? Haven't we shown you hospitality and kindness? It's late. Please let us close up and come as our guests another night. I implore you, he said, his hands in prayer in front of his face.

The captain stood and raised his rifle, pointing the barrel at the manager's face.

Are you harboring or do you know of any Confederate soldiers in the area? the captain asked.

No, said the manager. No, please, no. I'm a working man. I have a family.

Why don't you all get out of the building, said the captain, turning in a circle on his boot-heel. We thank you for your loyalty to the Union.

The bartender grabbed Martha, carried her out of the saloon and dropped her in her saddle. He untied her horse and handed her the reins. Get home as quick as you can; you shouldn't be out at night. Let your father get himself home from now on, he hissed.

Confused, Martha let her horse pace in place for a minute. Two of the men dragged the manager and threw him down, unresisting, in the road. From the line of horses waiting for them the men drew torches out of supply packs. They lit the torches and then they lit the saloon. It was an old building, made of dry planks, and in the sudden rising wind it caught like a match. Martha held her panicking horse tight and rode her away down the street. From there she watched the fire light the clouds. She could see the manager in silhouette, standing and gesticulating, clutching his head and crying as the walls of the building buckled and with a great sigh the roof slid away.

Miette

||||||||||||||||||||||||||||||||||||||||||||||

Umh! Umh-hm, said the man who joined me outside of Rosebud where we started onto the Gleichen Trail.

I asked him, Do you know a place called Deadwood?

He said, That is the very place I am going. Why are you going to Deadwood, if you don't mind my asking?

I'm going to find my mother.

He was on foot and lame and he refused to share my horse. He was old and I could not leave him behind, so I decided to walk beside him and lead her by the reins.

The river valley was rife with wild rose bushes in full bloom. Hundreds of doting pink faces filled my gaze, almost magical. The air was sweetened. In the sunlight the shimmering river dissolved and resolved itself before my eyes.

His shoulder and mine bumped every other step; that was how close we were. I looked at his face, so like a shriveled apple. His jaw wobbled and bobbed as he walked and a lump on his neck stood out like the moon emerging from behind a tree. His stooped shoulders were barely traceable beneath his shirt. He shambled along, dragging one turned-in foot.

She'll be happy to see you! he said. Umh! Whoever you are she will be happy to see you.

Why are you going to Deadwood? I asked him.

He shrugged and gestured to the sky. I'm just going, he said. Just keep moving. Thought of walking to Montana. Thought of walking there. Thought it would be too bumpy.

Bumpy?

Yes, bumpy, with all the mountains. Ain't got the right shoes.

We walked on together while I tried to think of what I should do for the man.

What does your mother look like? he asked at last.

I never met her.

Well then, you won't know her, will you? She could be any woman at all.

I know her name.

What is her name?

Martha, but people call her Calamity Jane.

He stopped walking at that and stared at me.

The wind rose up very strangely. I heard thunder roll and then, as if after a breath, the sky began to hail.

Come on, keep moving, I said. Crazy weather.

The hail was painful, as large as musket balls. The flowers were abused. I saw a blackbird knocked out of a tree and killed. We shouldered the wind with our faces tucked to our chests. Even my horse walked with her head swinging back and forth to escape the stinging. I took for granted that we were still heading in the right direction because it hurt too much to open my eyes and look around. Then, as suddenly as the hail began, it fell away and a blazing white sun took over the sky.

I know her, he said. I know your mother. Look, you see that hill, and those cliffs? He pointed at the landscape but there was nothing like what he described before us. The little man shook with excitement.

I know her, he exclaimed. She lived right behind there. Now turn this way. You see the brow of that hill, where it cuts the sky? Now look hard. Look hard to see it. And back this way. You see that ridge, so far away you can barely see it? You see that broken tree? Well, end to end, your famous mother owned every speck of this land. Owned it with her body for patrolling it as a scout and seeing and knowing it. Every tree and stone and animal that crossed this earth belonged to her. All of us were her sons and daughters brought into this world drunk and rolling on straw mats. And the real joke of it is our fathers carried each of us to be baptized, and we only knew a father's arms. Not one of us was baptized on her land. It was that way with you as well, wasn't it?

What the hell are you talking about?

Calamity Jane is my mother too.

He laughed and I shivered. A murder of crows the size of terriers came cawing over a break in the rocks and blackened the sky. I looked at the glittering balls of ice on the trail and I felt like I was sinking into a pure cold fire. I thought, he is either a lunatic or a ghost. If this is death, if I am somehow dead, then I will have to ask the Devil for a blanket. I looked at him and thought maybe the sudden hail pounding our heads was queering either what he said or what I heard or both, or else my grief had conjured a hallucination.

You know her?

I did but she's dead. Calamity Jane has been dead for years. A train hit her when she was drunk and sleeping on the tracks. Cut her into squirming parts and never stopped. The woman was living bile—living, moving, humping bile. But I think about her at Christmas.

He whipped out a long knife from his hip and struck my horse with the flat of the blade. She went stumbling fast down the incline. Her reins pulled from my hand and I had to chase her even though our six legs were made of unjointed lead.

Martha

||||||||||||||||||||||||||||||||||||||||||||||

S HE FLOATED IN THE WATER IN THE WEEDY CREEK, parched skin gleaming. Boys in uniform called abuse from the shore. She laughed and showed her finger. They dropped belts and guns and clothing in the long grasses and entered the water splashing like dogs, paddling to her. It was as if for an hour the war meant nothing. Martha and the other soldiers dove under the surface, touched the stones, scratched the soft silt and swam in circles. The cold water washed old dirt from wounds, erased false lines from their soft faces. Kicking, they felt feet and legs touch weeds. Empty stomachs rumbled.

She looked down at herself and then at them, how thin they all were. She turned her face towards the sun and touched the part in her hair where the scalp had burnt. She bent her knees, pulling herself under the surface. Water filled her ears and she heard the roaring.

Miette

||||||||||||||||||||||||||||||||||||||||||||||

T HEY CALLED IT OBLATION. IT BEGAN IN THE EAST but when it came to the West, the practice of leaving infants on the steps of monasteries, or in churches, or by cemetery graves had become the very incarnation of gifting a life to God.

I was an oblate?

Yes, you were a gift. St. Benedictine said that if a child—like you—Miette, should be donated to the service of God, then the child's hands should be wrapped and in one hand a petition should be placed so that the parents' intentions would be clear. These were not unwanted children; they were the offspring of noble families.

Father, I wish I were yours. I wish—

Shh, you don't understand what that would mean.

T HERE WAS no town at all behind the hills where the crazy man who hit my horse and claimed to be my brother had pointed. I saw no one on the trail after him until I arrived at a hamlet in magic hour.

The low sun shone more yellow on the walls of the houses as the pink sky deepened and the heat began to lift. Certain birds sing at different times of the day but the birds that sing at magic hour are all like doves, cooing. Even the molting ravens sound like cooing doves if they make a noise at all. Though I heard children laughing, hidden behind walls in the yards of their houses, the place where I stopped (I did not know what it was called) seemed hushed as if the roofs had absorbed the last human energy of the day along with the red stains of sunset. My footsteps echoed on the cobbled paving stones of the main street. I felt quite suddenly all right, no longer wondering about the ravings of the crazy stranger who had cursed my mother dead and hit my horse. I released him completely from whatever ill he meant me and said a little prayer for his health.

The picture of my father I carried in my pocket began to sweat with the heat until it was almost like he himself was sweating up against my heart. I took it out and studied it. It was an old photo, ragged all around the edges, riddled with pinpricks from where I had posted it many times, and with a hole the size of a pencil where the paper had decayed. It was the only image I had ever seen of him before he took the robes. I had found it in a flowerpot filled up with herbs: dried lemon balm, castilla blossoms, rue. I took it without telling him and pinned it inside my dresser drawer.

He was sitting in front of a bookcase in a suit and tie and hat. His moustache and sideburns looked fuller and darker than I had ever seen them. He looked like a man that women might have conspired to be near in the dusty summer hours. But stiff and so still because he couldn't move for the picture, and that made him a stranger, for I never saw him alive when he wasn't moving, farming, hiking, hammering, digging a grave, or soothing something. He was restless and he liked to be away from people but maybe that is what it takes to be a man devoted to God in a place where you build and rebuild Heaven alone. I touched my pocket and wondered if the picture would help my mother to remember the young priest she saw that day she surrendered my little self.

All the doors to all the houses were shut, which was strange when any breeze was worth gold. A few doorways were overgrown with weeds. When we were about to reach the edge of town I saw an old woman, wrapped in a coarse dark shawl, cross the street ahead some ways. I saw her long loose white hair picked at by the wind, and then I didn't see her and then I blinked a few times and saw her again cross the street in the other direction. Finally, a person, I thought.

Evening, I called out. Evening—where am I?

She stopped in the middle of the street and looked at me. Heaven, she said.

What?

Only a joke. This is Enchant, she said.

I calculated how long we had been walking the streets and not seeing anyone and I thought, I must be dreaming. But when I tested the smell of the air and I stomped my feet in the dust it seemed as if, in spite of the absence of children or birds to match the sounds I could hear, and in spite of the blue shadows creeping over the doorways burdened with weeds, the town felt alive. I looked at the woman, who had stayed in the middle of the street, and her mouth was full of teeth and her eyes blinked the way that living eyes blink. I had been so long used to silence. For a year my father had been so ill and I had driven away other chatty people to spend my life with my horse or with my father or with books. I had spent so much time being carried over the earth or as a bodiless person treading through memories and stories, I did not know much about real bodies, how solid they were or what size they should be. So when this woman spoke again and pointed I just went where she told me, to a house beside a bridge. I knocked on the door and the woman walked up behind me, opened the door, went inside, closed it, then opened it again and said hello.

Where can I find lodging? I asked her.

You can stay here. I knew you were coming. Your father told me.

My father? My father is dead.

That must be why his voice was so weak. She shrugged. If you're looking, you may find someone still among the living tomorrow. You have nothing to lose by taking a look around. What are you called?

My name is Miette, I told her, although my name is Martha after my mother. Only my father called me Miette and then only when we were alone. Little crumb, it means in French, sweet little thing. It made me happy every time he said my name.

IN THE house it was as if she had been waiting with everything prepared for me. New candles were so freshly cut and lit in the dining room that the wicks still flared. Two places were set at the table. Baskets of breads and fruit and plates of meat were arranged between the settings. A chipped green vase held wildflowers that strangely had no scent. That she had done all this within the second or two of closing the door and then opening it again was impossible. I heard music and I saw by the table a large stand on which sat a black box with a bugle sticking out of it. A tan cylinder rotated, horizontal, on top of the box. Music strained out of the wide brass mouth of the bugle, a human voice singing some song. It was in French.

It's Creole music, she said, when she saw me looking at it. It's a Louis Moreau Gottschalk song. Haven't you ever seen a phonograph before?

I shook my head, no. The only music I knew were songs the Blackfoot sang, and hymns.

She laughed and motioned me into a dark hall where I could barely discern the doorways from the rest of the walls. By the light from the candles on the table behind me I could see bulky shadows loom in otherwise empty rooms, cast by what I could not tell.

I'm a friend of your father, she said. I have some of his things here. People leave me their things. They stop here on the way to somewhere else and leave behind things for me to store but they never come back. I have had to burn my own furniture to make room for all the odds and ends that people left. I'll fix you a good mattress and you can stay in the room where I have his belongings. I think he left a bed, a pillow and a chest.

My father stayed here?

Yes, he stayed here on his way to the church. We were close friends. How is he?

He died.

You said that. He must have thought I had forsaken him. We always promised that we would see each other again and take the last steps of life together. We were the best of friends. Did he ever talk about me?

No. Are you sure you mean my father?

I drew his picture from my pocket and showed it to her.

She smiled and grabbed the little picture and kissed it.

Then she held it to her nose and smelled the fading herbs and melting chemicals and my sweat.

Yes. That's him. I went with him the day this photo was taken. I said, You should have a picture of yourself so you can remember what you looked like before you left me behind. He was here getting ready to cross the border into Heaven. He crossed a few times before he stayed away. Of course, that was years ago and I was a young girl being wicked. I loved him very much. I loved him very, very much and I ask myself sometimes if I might have married if I'd never met him. I ask myself about the true nature of that deep love. When you let yourself feel that much you ruin your chances of a happy marriage.

She sighed and handed me back the picture.

So, he's dead, she said. That's strange. He was so pretty, and so *sweet*. It made a person want to love him. It made a person happy to love him. Well, I will catch up to him. I know a few shortcuts to Heaven and God owes me a small favor. I'm sorry, I'm sorry, I shouldn't speak to you like this. It's only that you're his daughter and so it feels to me as if you might have been my daughter.

He adopted me.

Of course he did.

It was clear to me by now that she was insane. Loneliness had turned her empty rooms into storage for the phantom belongings of people she may or may not have ever known. When we reached the room she meant for me she opened the door and inside there was no bed, no chest, no furnishings of any kind. On the ledge of the open window was a small stack of books holding back the frayed curtain. She left me there and I unpacked my sleeping bag. After a minute I went to the window and picked up one of the books. I turned it over in my hand, stroked the spine, felt the leather cover, set it down. I went back to my pack and took out the one possession of my father's I had been unable to leave behind. It was a copy of Jules Verne's novel *Five Weeks in a Balloon.* I knew it, every chocolaty French word, and I knew the signature on the inside leaf.

I sat and fell in love again with the words and the voice I remembered. How I loved the unicorn-shaped balloon, half full, rising with the trade winds to travel across Africa. I climbed into my sleeping bag, pulled it up to my neck and read, listening to my father as if he lived in me. I could not count how many nights he wasted candles reading me to sleep. And in the mornings I would translate the story and write it out in a notebook. I translated to myself again, here in the semi-darkness, remembering at once his voice:

> One must never forget how fragile, the equilibrium of a balloon, floating in the atmosphere. The loss of what seems an almost insignificant weight is enough to displace the thing and send it up into dangerous altitudes. But the doctor knew well how many pounds to carry and how slowly to consume fuel and food and brandy.
>
> Nor did he forget an awning to shelter the wicker car, reinforced with steel. Nor did he forget to count the coverings and blankets, all the bedding of the journey, nor some fowling pieces and rifles, with their spare supply of powder and ball.
>
> Here is the summing up of his various items, and their weights:

FERGUSON, 135 POUNDS
KENNEDY, 153
JOE, 120
WEIGHT OF THE MAIN BALLOON, 650
WEIGHT OF THE SECONDARY BALLOON, 510
CAR AND NETWORK, 280
ANCHORS, INSTRUMENTS, AWNINGS, AND SUNDRY INCLUD-
    ING UTENSILS, GUNS, COVERINGS, ETC., 190
DRIED MEAT, PEMMICAN, BISCUITS, TEA,
    COFFEE, BRANDY, 386
WATER, 400
APPARATUS, 700
WEIGHT OF THE HYDROGEN, 276
BALLAST, 200
TOTAL: 4,000 POUNDS

Four thousand pounds floating over lions and boars and wildebeests!

Yes, Miette. That's enough for tonight. Tomorrow we'll read more. Let me pray with you before you sleep. He closed the book and kneeled beside me.

HE HAD always held the book. The weight of it in my hands was new. I sniffed it and flipped through the pages. Near the back was a folded piece of paper, tucked in, separating chapters. I opened it and read:

Dear Sir or Father or Brother,

I know a man who knows you and he says you are good and he is a very good man so I believe it.

I have a baby inside me who will be coming out

soon. It is the child of Wild Bill Hickok who I love more than horses. If it is a boy he should be named James, for that is Bill's name, and if it is a girl, then Martha after me. You are a thousand miles away but I will ride to meet you at the border if you will take this one. I am no mother, except that I know enough to get out of the mothering business. I know you live in the Badlands in Canada and I live in the Badlands in South Dakota so maybe it is something like home. I know you are a wandering bishop and so I think I understand you better than other religious men who think they can never be wrong. I am often wrong but I consider it a strength to say so. I don't know this one inside me at all, but I want to find a home for it far away from me with good sober people who will love it and keep it safe.

Please send me some word and tell me if you will take my baby and call it an orphan. And if you take this one, please don't teach it to speak French. I don't want it to grow up crazy.

Sincerely,
Martha Canary

He left everything in this room his last time through here.

I looked up and the woman was in my doorway. She was in a nightgown that made her look like a rag doll.

What time? I said, while I recovered myself and pushed down a sudden swell of anger at her for spying on me in the dark.

Keep them. There are more secrets in those odds of furniture than I can decipher.

Thank you but I can't take the furniture.

He left them the time he came to get you. You were two months old and half dead, wrinkled and thin and yellow. We spent every minute trying to get some water into you. Your mother rode with you tied to her back. Your face was in the sun and she didn't stop even once to feed you. She was the ugliest woman I ever saw, tall and filthy, and she smelled like liquor. I couldn't ever imagine who would make love to her.

I sucked on my tongue and then said, I don't believe you.

Suit yourself, she said and shrugged and left.

I silently cursed her a liar and named her Hag. I heard her singing a lullaby to herself deep in the darkened house.

Hush-a-bye, don't you cry
Go to sleep, my little baby
When you wake, you shall have cake
And all the pretty little horses
Blacks and bays, dapple and grays
All the pretty little horses
And mama loves and daddy loves
Oh they love their little baby
When you wake, you shall have cake
And all the pretty little horses
Blacks and bays, dapple and grays
All the pretty little horses
Blacks and bays, dapple and grays
Coach and six white horses
Way down yonder, down in the meadow
Lies a poor little child

The bees and the flies are pickin' out its eyes
The poor little child crying for its mother
Oh, crying for its mother
Hush-a-bye, don't you cry
Go to sleep, you little baby
When you wake, you shall have cake
And all the pretty little horses
Blacks and bays, dapple and grays
Coach and six white horses
Blacks and bays, dapple and grays
All the pretty little horses.

Martha

||||||||||||||||||||||||||||||||||||||||||||

S OME SAID SHE WAS A HIGHWAYMAN, A ROAD AGENT, that she was involved with opium running, that she led gangs of Indians to lynch white men prospecting in the sacred hills. It can be said, wrote one skinny upstart, that Calamity Jane knows more about jail than about scouting, trooping or even bullwhacking.

S HE WAS known to liberate horses. After quarreling with one husband, Steer, who beat her, hit her in the lip with a rock and tried to stab her, she tried to get him arrested. When that didn't work, when he beat her again with the heel of his boot, she tied him to a mule and left him in a stable. She took his saddle and his horse and rode right out of marriage.

S HE ARRIVED in Rawlins to see the swinging bodies of Jim Lacy and Opium Bob. Reporters crowded around her and scribbled on their pads. She called the sight of the two dead men in the middle of the town *seeing the elephant*, which meant reaching one's destination, witnessing a flood or an epidemic, or encountering something that makes you go back the way that you came.

SHE TOLD a reporter who was sure he had her pinned for a stagecoach robbery that it might have been the night she married Jesse James.

It was a night for madness, she said.

A MAN named Maguire walked the streets of Deadwood handing out a colorful pamphlet to tourists. The pamphlet described the first time he saw her:

> I saw a GIRL in neat-fitting gaiters, a coat, panta-loons of buckskin, a vest of fur-trimmed antelope skin, and a broad-brimmed Spanish hat on the back of a bucking angry animal. She hung onto the beast. She threw herself from side to side. She hollared a war-whoop, and patted its neck. She rode that beast of Hell on up over the gulch, over ditches and through reservoir and mudholes, praising it through its fury, until it damned well gave in and loved her. I didn't ever see no other such an animal turned from demon to angel.

IN CHEYENNE the newspaper editor was so afraid of her that when she arrived in town and marched into his office to tell him to make his journalists stop printing lies he escaped through the skylight, leaving his trembling adolescent son to take down this message:

> Print in the Leader that Calamity Jane, the child of the Regiment and pioneer white woman of the Black Hills, is in Cheyenne, or I'll scalp you alive, and

hang you to a telegraph pole. You hear me and you
don't forget it.

Calamity Jane

RIDING THROUGH Wyoming, into a remote mining camp,
she found miners beaten and starving, their food, their
horses and their equipment stolen by road agents, and themselves left without boots to figure a long trek over stony land
to help. She rode to a grocery store ten miles away. She told
the owner that men were dying and she needed help. He was
intractable, arms folded over a big belly framed by suspenders. On the counter she saw a novel, placed down open-faced.
She smiled.

Do you know who I am?

He looked at her and he looked down at the book's cover and
he looked back at the guns strapped to her body.

Who am I? she asked.

She returned to the camp with food and blankets.

The storeowner became famous for being robbed by the
Heroine of Whoop-Up.

SHE APPEARED in paintings and prints as a heroically pretty
girl with flowing hair and dark-lined eyes, or else first as a
man and then as a woman. Songs were written about her or
adapted to refer to her. She sometimes sang those songs to
herself as she drifted between states. She liked "Crazy Jane,"
but more often she sang the one that sounded ideal.

Jane was a farmer's daughter,
The fairest one of three,

Love in his arms had caught her,
As fast as fast cou'd be;
William was a soldier,
As brave as brave cou'd be,
And he resolv'd to marry,
The fairest one of three,
The fairest one of three,
The fairest one of three,
And he resolv'd to marry,
The fairest one of three.

Lena thought it wiser,
A rich man's wife to be,
And so she took a Miser
As old as old cou'd be,
Annie felt Love's passion,
But wish'd this world to see
So chose a Lad of Fashion,
The dullest of the three,
The dullest of the three,
The dullest of the three,
So chose a Lad of Fashion,
The dullest of the three.

Lena's spouse perplext her,
A widow soon was she,
Annie's liv'd and vext her
As well as well cou'd be.
But Jane possest true pleasure
With one of low degree,
They were each other's treasure

The happiest of the three,
The happiest of the three,
The happiest of the three,
They were each other's treasure
The happiest of the three.

Miette

‖‖

I WOKE BEFORE THE HAG AND WENT OUTSIDE TO USE the privy. Water dripping from the roof tiles gouged cups of mud out of the earth around the stone patio. The night was short and the morning air tasted new. I was sitting on the pot staring at a leaf stuck in one of the cups of mud; it startled every time a drop struck it. A storm had passed without me knowing it. Ragged hens huddled nearby on a roost, shivering to get the water off their feathers. I watched the clouds retreat and the spiteful sun emerge to send shocks of heat down on the rocks, which sparkled like the backs of frogs.

What's taking you so long on the privy, girl?

Nothing.

If you stay there too long a snake will come and bite you.

Go away, I muttered. Leave me alone.

She left me and I retreated into memories of an old friend, the Blackfoot woman my father called Zita after his sister and after the saint who had angels bake bread for her while she tended to people in need. I worked at a memory of flying kites on windy days. The three of us ran beneath the volcanic-looking columns of hoodoos.

Those are bad mothers, she said of the hoodoos. They were turned to stone and their heads were knocked off.

I was jealous of Zita's children. I needed her so much that I hid the kites when they tried to play. Zita sent them running home.

When the wind pulled too hard I called, help me! She put her hands over mine and together we tugged the somersaulting kite back from the sky. My father with his green eyes like glistening bottle-glass laughed at us wading in the long prairie grass.

He squeezed my hand as we walked.

Zita sent her children home, I said. He nodded.

I looked up and saw the Hag in the doorway again. I felt a snap between my eyes and I had to dig my nails into the palms of my hands to keep from screaming at her.

It's called a privy because that's where people go to have some privacy, I said.

Did your father teach you to speak that way?

No, ma'am.

If you're done at that thing, empty it out and wash up and come help me shell some corn.

I have to be goin', ma'am.

Well, when you are done goin', come help me.

So I lingered as long as I could and then came in to help her. I felt that was my duty since she had let me stay the night.

It's fifty miles to Lethbridge, she said when I came in. Should take you a day or a day and a half depending on your pace. From there you can cross the border at Coutts into Sweetgrass. What's your horse's name? she asked. She was looking out the window.

I don't know.

She's not yours, then?

She's mine.

Then why doesn't she have a name? A pretty brown thing like that a person wants to name.

I took her from someone. He knows her name.

You stole that horse.

He was whipping her. He whipped her with a chain and then he left her outside a bar and I took her away. He didn't deserve a horse.

She sighed and crossed herself. Did your father know?

No. He was already sick.

And the man did not come after his horse?

He came after her. I sent him away.

Your father was weak for horses too, she said.

The corn was all shelled. I looked over her shoulder at my horse. She's more black than brown, I thought, with eyelashes long enough to make a breeze.

Am I pretty? I said before I could stop myself. As if to show how strange my query, a hummingbird paused at my eye level just outside the window, attracted by the heavy purple blossoms of cut jasmine in a vase on the sill. The woman looked at me. Behind her, on a shelf nailed to the wall, was a porcelain portrait of the Sacred Heart. Beside it hung a Catholic calendar with all the ferial and Ember days, the fish days and the feast days, and the seasons marked. I felt hot, afraid. I looked down on my shaking hands.

No, she whispered sadly. Her face was transparent with pity. You're not pretty. Your mother wasn't pretty either. But, she said and sighed, I heard that she loved animals too. Once she caught a man whipping a mule and she rode over to him and told him to stop. He cracked the whip at her head and sent her hat flying into the dirt. She drew a rifle on him and said, You put that back where you found it. And he did.

How do you know that story?

The woman is famous. Everyone knows one thing about her.

I don't.

Well, now you do, she said. You should go home. She's probably long gone.

I promised him.

Yes. She nodded and sighed. She moved to a drawer under the counter and drew out a folded garment. She held the shoulders and let the rest fall until I could see it was a dress of black crepe with a high neck and buttons to the waist.

Take this, she said. Wear it when you tell your mother that the man she gave her child to is dead now.

I RODE away with the dress in my side-pack. It began to rain again. I listened to the water in the creek winding beside us, mumbling and gurgling in harmony with my stomach. My hat kept slipping over my eyes. I took it off, shook off the water and kept it on my lap. The raindrops threaded down my cheeks like tears. In the hours that passed I began to hear voices, the Hag saying, Yes, I nearly was your mother, didn't you know? The man on the trail saying, She's living, moving, humping bile! My father saying the Rosary, asking for the forgiveness of sins and the resurrection of the flesh. I heard beads clicking as they rolled against one another. After a while the voices were speaking together and I started talking to my horse to drown them out.

I don't know why but in the middle of the night I put that black dress on and lay on the ground in the grass, watching the stars fall. The heat from my fire was almost gone. I was waiting for the last embers to die. My horse was asleep.

A voice said: I took on everything that happened, as if I

wanted it just the way it happened. That was my trick. That was a good trick.

I turned my head. I did not know the voice but I knew who it was. I'm dreaming you, I said, although there was no one there that I could see. There was nothing but smoke from the broken fire and a strange smell of whisky.

Yes, the voice whispered. When the drunk hit I threw back my head and howled. That's when they knew to hand me a bottle and escort me from the bar. And then I walked for as long as I could, which was never very long, until I was away from them, and then I fell on my knees and I howled.

I hate you, I said. The night was already so far gone that I didn't mind talking angry and crazy to myself. Why did you give me away? What did you think would happen to me? Didn't you care what happened to me?

The wind blew ashes into my eyes. I felt very sorry for the girl that was me.

Go away, I said. Go away. I'll look for you but I don't care if I find you.

I forced myself back to my father, back into recollection. It gave me peace even in the black cold night without anyone alive to love me. I remembered how when he read to me and I was cold he would spread his much-mended, oldest, wool cassock over my sheets and tuck the black cloth all around my body. It may have been a sin for him to use his old robes as a blanket, but I knew that he could never put away in the dark dusty cupboard his first and most precious vestments. I felt a hard nut form in my chest for he was a good man, a really good man, and I could remember his voice perfectly, but for how long?

He read softly in the dark:

I intend not to be separated from my balloon until I reach the western coast of Africa. While we are together, every thing is possible. Without it, I fall back into danger and difficulty as well as the natural obstacles of such an expedition. Together with my balloon, neither heat, nor torrents, nor tempests, nor the simoom, nor unhealthy climates, nor wild animals, nor savage men, can frighten me! If I am too hot, I can ascend; if I am too cold, I can descend. I can pass over mountains; I can sweep across precipices; I can sail beyond rivers; I can rise above storms; I can skim torrents like a bird! I can advance without fatigue; I can halt without need of repose! I can soar above the sleeping cities! I can speed onward with the rapidity of a tornado, sometimes at the loftiest heights, sometimes only a hundred feet above the soil, while the map of Africa unrolls itself beneath my gaze in the great atlas of the world.

I love you.

Go to sleep, Mighty Miette. Go to sleep.

I LAY in the dirt by the trail trying to see things that were close to me, my horse, my arm, the firepit, but I could only see things that were millions of miles above. The round ceiling of stars shone through thin clouds. I wiped my cheeks with impatient hands and tasted grit in my teeth. Below the stars but far, far above everything else, Father, you were hiding. Hiding in God's immensity. Hiding where I could not see you and where my prayers could not reach your ears.

Martha

||||||||||||||||||||||||||||||||||||||||||||||||

SHE CHANGED THINGS WHEN SHE ENTERED THE room. She made the other patrons excited about the scene that might come, nervous about being the center of a future joke, irritated by the interruption. She didn't do anything. She ordered drinks and she drank them and in doing so she became drunk. Every few times she got odd and said odd things. She was often too affectionate, greeting strangers, hello, dear, and, hello, darling, or too aggressive, accusing bystanders of staring at her or judging her. When the temperance ladies rallied outside the Gem singing, King Alcohol is very sly; a liar from the first. He'll make you drink until you're dry, then drink, because you thirst!, she roared back, The spinsters will be ministers when pigs begin to fly! Then she carried a tray of whiskies into the group and offered every lady a glass of spirits.

Still, she was neither as amorous nor as aggressive as Bill, who drank as much or more than her on many of the same nights.

Miette

|||||||||||||||||||||||||||||||||||||||||||

BESIDES FORKS AND TINS AND JARS, HEXAGONAL pencils riddled with bite marks, the odd piece of cotton, broken books all trampled into cart and horse tracks, I also passed the damaged coffins of three children beside the trail. The broken wood allowed a view of their dusty, wrapped bodies. One coffin, two feet long, was turned on its side and a coyote stood, pulling the cloth through the bottom. He looked up at me and then turned back to his task. My stomach twisted but I rode past. The little bones had no protection. Like the fossils of ancient civilizations the bodies of these children were too delicate, too fragile to leave a final imprint, too light even to stay in the ground.

At midday we stopped to rest. I sat cross-legged in the grass, shredding grass between my nails, making whistles of the wider blades and blowing them tunelessly. I read Jules Verne for a while, shading the pages with my body by lying on my stomach propped up on my elbows. I fantasized that lying this way I was invisible to all but the birds. I loved the chapter summaries, the way they lined up my expectations.

Thirty-Second. The Capital of Bornou. The Islands of the Biddiomahs. The Condors. The Doctor's Anxieties. His Precautions. An Attack in Mid-air. The Balloon

Covering Torn. The Fall. Sublime Self-Sacrifice. The Northern Coast of the Lake.

When my stomach growled and my elbows and neck ached I sat up and chewed on some bread so stale it cut my tongue. Antelope grazed fearlessly around me. Wild lilac blued the edges of my vision. After some time staring at the sky I saw a cloud that looked like a roast chicken so I set up a fire.

WE RODE on the long next day. Herds of wild horses watched us pass. An immense murmuration of starlings spun across the horizon. The birds were a flowing black powder, thousands together in a wave taking on the shape of one much greater thing, a hand reaching down from the sky to conduct music.

A buggy carrying a high pile of boxes and pieces of stove-pipes and blankets passed us going the other way. The driver was an official-looking gentleman. His neat little body in its dark suit jolted and jostled with every bump in the road. He waved to me and I waved back.

At dusk the bats and nighthawks waltzed overhead while I unrolled my pack. I thought of doing some target practice with an empty can but did not want to waste bullets. I cooked myself some beans over the fire and enjoyed them with the corn that Mrs. Nixon had packed for me. I watched the stars light up through the woodsmoke.

I fell asleep wrapped in my blankets on the open hillside and I slept deeply until once again it rained, rained in this most arid place! I woke up being pecked by water and saw the lightning flash. I set up my tent and crawled into the darkness. In the thunder was my father's voice, but this time I knew it was only my ache to hear him.

Martha

|||||||||||||||||||||||||||||||||||||||||||||

I T WAS 1862 AND THE CIVIL WAR WAS ON. IN WASH-
ington, on September 20th, President Abraham Lincoln
wept over the body of his eleven-year-old son, dead from
drinking the polluted water that ran from the taps in the
White House. In Virginia City, Martha and her sisters
appeared for the first time in the newspapers as a band of
vagrant children, a social concern, begging door to door.
When not begging, Martha hid her sisters and brothers in
bushes, under wagons, wherever she could, out of sight of
troopers in homespun uniforms who would not hesitate to
hang vagrants, even children, with their own belts. Evenings,
Martha held her mother's hand while she lolled drunk upon
the floor of the shanty. It was Martha who trod to the gambling
hall to collect her father. It was Martha who slept on the floor to
give an unwanted, armed guest her bed. Afternoons, she swept
neighbors' houses to earn money for food and cough medi-
cine. Whenever she could she followed the cowboys and
watched them practice throwing a rope, shooting at targets,
jumping from the back of a horse onto the fleeing body of a
calf. Once in a while they let her ride an old pony and help to
drive the cattle home.

SHE WENT to the post office with her brother Elijah to mail a letter for their mother. They were excited for the treat of seeing bright stamps from around the world on display. The open books under glass were all from the postmaster's collection. They bumped into each other rushing through the door, and stopped.

There was a war ad in the post office that showed Winfield Scott, a Mexican war hero from Virginia, as the Hercules of the Union slaying the Great Dragon of Secession. Scott was in his uniform, which was like a short dress with a billowing skirt. His shoulders were adorned with epaulets. His hair was crimped and neat. He wore tall shiny black boots and a belt that bore a pattern of gold leaves against a black background. He brandished a club, holding it with two hands above one shoulder. The club was the length of his upper body and roughly hewn. It was labeled Liberty Union. Scott's expression was that of a man gravely assuming an unfortunate duty. He gazed impassively at the hydra, whose fat tail wound between his legs. Each head was a finely drawn portrait of a Confederate leader, labeled on the collar for those who might presume an accidental likeness. Floyd was bent over backwards but the other heads stared at the club. Along each of the serpentine throats that joined the human faces to one monstrous body (labeled Secession) was written a Confederate crime. The first neck read Robbery; the second read Extortion. The third neck read Treason. The fourth read Perjury. Then came Piracy, Lying, Hatred and Blasphemy.

Martha and Elijah were nine and seven, looking up at the poster, the letters they had been sent to post forgotten in their hands.

They think we're monsters. They want to kill us, Elijah said.

Miette

||||||||||||||||||||||||||||||||||||||||||||

Father, I have sinned.

I hovered behind the screen of the back door as my father took confession from Zita's youngest, her smallest daughter, in the main room. She wore a dark blouse and leggings under a white ruffled apron dress so I knew she had come directly from the mission. She knelt on the rough wood floor behind the folding screen. A yellow medallion on a chain shone at the base of her throat. My father sat in his chair with his back to her and his arms folded across his chest, nodding.

Father, this man, she whispered. He breaks horses. He sticks to their backs like he is covered in burrs. I watched him and I had bad thoughts. Like the thoughts my sister talks about with the older girls. My brother told me to stay away from him. My brother said that this man could pull up dreams out of your stomach and make you do things. My mother does not know, Father.

I will not share your confession.

I believed him when he said he was a tamer, Father, a kind of doctor for women's wildness. I saw him put his hand on my sister's stomach and how still she stood. And he did that to me too; he put his hand on my stomach. But I didn't feel still, I felt like wiggling. He rubbed my stomach and then he moved his hands away and when I thought I would cry he took my hands and stroked my fingers. He rubbed my wrists and my forearms and he started telling me my fortune. He said that I would have many lovers and I would break all their hearts. He said I would die from consumption before I was twenty. He said that only my first lover would ever reach the deepest parts of me. And somehow he ended up stark naked.

Child, Mary, you can't be more than ten years old. You can't even have begun to bleed?

Yes, Father, I began this summer. My brother said later that this is what the man did with every girl and he did it so often that sometimes it worked. I knew that it was dangerous to lie with him because the moon was wrong. But, Father, I had so much bad courage in the dark.

My father rubbed the heels of his hands hard on his knees as he breathed out ragged and loud. He gave her the requisite instructions for penance but when she finished he went to his bookshelf and drew off a book I had never seen before and he took money from the center of that book and folded it into her palm.

Tell your mother I owe her this and more, he said, for helping with Martha.

The next day I listened to him argue with a man who was helping a neighbor. I listened to an argument that never betrayed its point and so was pointless. When the man walked away my father held onto the knot in his cincture looking like he could hurt someone. But he couldn't.

I HAD meant to ride until the dark stopped me but a storm, and with it sudden night, forced me to set up camp while my horse pawed the ground and thrashed her head about. Snorts and the clattering of her teeth were interrupted by low, disturbed whinnies. She backed up against her reins and tried to pull free from the little tree where she was tied. When sheet lightning rendered the scene I could see that her eyes were wild, the whites bright in her face. I left my tent and stood in the cracking darkness wiping waves of water from her neck, holding her head still, blocking her when she wanted to plunge, rubbing her face and pulling her ears so she would listen to me. Long rolls of sound vibrated the earth underfoot. The shadowy tree branches waved overhead. My fingers grew stiff until I couldn't unbend them. I slept leaning into her, starting each time she shook or swayed.

A stiff bark woke me. I shook rain from my face and looked around, straining at the darkness. My hands were numb and blue, hooked into the reins, and my arms, neck and back were full of stinging nettles. In flashes, near the sodden handkerchief of my tent, I saw a long body. I felt sick and my vision failed for a second. The curvature and the length of the figure suggested the body of a large woman. But the neck was too thick, too long. I pulled my hands free. They were useless. I crept forward and saw the graceful head, the eyes open and frozen, and the great dark gash across the cheek. My boot touched the fresh blood of a killed deer.

I shook my arms and bit my hands until they were mine again. I looped a noose around the deer's neck and threw the other end of the rope over a high thick branch and with the leverage of another tree I hung the deer until I heard a crack and saw her overhead. I tied her off, and moved our camp as far as I dared in the dark. In spite of gratitude and hunger, I did not want to be beside a dead deer when whatever barked in the night returned for its dinner.

A few hours later, in the morning, I stepped out and saw ravens squalling in the sky. I left my horse and walked with the saddlebag that contained my knife and hatchet and some rope back to the deer. She was young and healthy-looking. I searched for a rock about the size of a finch's body. I looked the deer over carefully and then I cut the skin around her neck and pulled it down until I could put the rock under the skin and tie it off tightly, making a kind of a hitch. Then I cut off her lower legs, holding them against the tree and using the hatchet. I sliced the skin up her legs to her underside and made sure she was cut all the way to the neck. Then I tied more rope around the hitch I had made in her skin and I went back to get my horse. It took a long bloody time to pull her skin off, but once the skin started it came off clean with a loud rip and lay like a discarded garment beneath her. I butchered the meat into small pieces and filled two bags with it. I draped the skin over my saddle.

When I was done there was still plenty left for Mr. Bear and Missus Wolf and all their coyote, fox and raven neighbors. I packed the bundles on the back of my horse with my other gear and we went looking for a smokehouse.

As I RODE into Lethbridge all the clean rich ladies riding shotgun in their husbands' Packards and Oldsmobiles down the wide roads stared at me as though I were a Hallowe'en apparition. They were like owls their heads rotated so. The sound of those cars. It felt so strange to look down on them. Blood seeping through the bags had stained my horse's sides and I had had no chance to wash after the butchering. I was covered in shades of blood. It amused me to take out my rifle and ride with it held across my saddle as if I were a gunfighter entering a frontier town.

I found the trading post in the center of town; it was a little wooden house with a tall brick false front in that top-hat style that suggests a second floor. I left my horse staring after me. The high sound of a little bell tripping gave away my entry. A woman was sorting accounts behind the counter. Around her were piss-pots and fry pans and top hats and saddles and canteens and jars of buttons and piles of socks and spools of belts, spotting scopes and stuffed parrots and bicycle parts and every sort of thing. A thick stack of dollar bills lay in a drawer before her that she shut quickly. She frowned at my appearance and I held up the deerskin.

If you are a bandit woman you have come to the wrong place. If you want to sell me that skin it has to be tanned. And if those are bags of meat and you are here to sell them then they have to be cured, dried or smoked. Which, by your meager look, I am guessing they are not. You can't just kill a beast and sling it around my place!

I meant no offense. Can you lend me the wood and screens to build a smokehouse and I'll smoke some meat for you? Or just tell me where to find one and I'll give you the skin for free, I offered.

She shook her head and turned her back on me. Her backside was half as broad as the counter. The walls were hidden behind racks of coats. An open armoire revealed a selection of wedding dresses and mourning suits. She pretended to be counting blankets, waiting for me to leave. The stack of blankets was neatly folded but she stroked and patted them as if soothing wrinkles from fine linen.

I can make do with a crate and a hammer and some old screen, I said. I'll give you half the meat.

She squared her shoulders, put her hands on her hips and turned back to me. She clucked her tongue and reached over her head to finger a vast swath of beaded necklaces, red, turquoise, white, yellow and pearl, hanging from a hook in a low beam. She assessed me and sighed.

Maybe I could help you if you were to buy something. I have some fresh imported Hutterite chicken. You look like you could use some meat.

What makes it Hutterite chicken? I asked.

She shrugged. Conversion, I suppose, and then betrayal. Have you got any salt? she asked.

I don't.

She pursed her lips and squinted at the weak sunlight. I'll give you a bag of salt if you'll help me do inventory. I don't want that skin, the cutting is ragged, it's not fleshed and it doesn't have a head.

I can go back and get the head.

I don't want the head. I want someone to inventory boots; the last time I did it there was a foot in one. Make yourself some brine and soak the meat and if it looks good I'll get you a smokehouse and if it tastes good I'll take half. But I need three days of work from you and I need your boots.

Where will I stay? I asked, feeling like I had wandered into a trap.

You have a horse?

Yes.

I suppose you need feed for your horse?

Yes.

Then I need four days of work and you can both sleep in my stable. I suppose you need food too, and a bath.

Five days work? I asked, and she nodded.

And your saddle. You'll need to buy back your boots and a saddle, I suppose?

Images of skeletons stacked in the hay of the stable floated in my mind. I need to think about it, I said, and I backed up all the way out the door. As I turned to leave I saw a pile of folded Confederate and Union uniforms topped by a tray of wedding bands beside a collection of Bibles.

Where you goin'? she called sharply.

Thank you. I won't bother you. I'm going to South Dakota.

That's a long lonely ride. Are you for mining?

No.

Are you gambling?

No.

You don't look like a whore, at least not a good one.

I'm looking for Calamity Jane. I have a message for her.

Ha! You're goin' the wrong way. Better go to Virginia City. Last time I read her name she was there.

I watched her hunt through papers but she did not find the proof of her direction. Exasperated she said, better yet, go anywhere you please. Here, I know what you'll want.

She turned to sift through another stack of papers.

Here it is. Here's a history of the woman. She's not even real. She's just the made-up fantasy of that little man.

She dropped a pamphlet before me. It was an illustrated biography of Ned Wheeler.

Twenty cents, she said, and that's to save you the cost of hunting phantoms.

I BOUGHT the book, bags of salt, dried herbs, a couple of screens and wood, and a tin bath from her. A man and wife offered me a room at the hotel in exchange for smoking some rabbits for them. The man giggled inconsolably at my appearance until the woman put him to bed with a bottle. I built a little smokehouse in the back and while I smoked the deer meat and the rabbits I read the brief story of a boy who dreamed of women. The story was written very plainly and the two illustrations were of Ned Wheeler himself and his first famous creation, the magical personage of Wild Edna.

The Inventive Ned Wheeler

||||||||||||||||||||||||||||||||||||||||||||||

NED WHEELER WAS BORN SICKLY IN UPSTATE NEW York. He grew up bookish and pale, dreaming of Western adventure. At twelve he wrote a short novel about a girl named Wild Edna who dressed in men's clothes and rode beside a man named Dangerous Joe. Wild Edna would shoot a fly out of the air if she thought that it might light upon Dangerous Joe. Ned wrote four more books from the point of view of a daring female. He read his stories to his mother every night when she came to tuck him in, sit beside him and take his temperature. Twasn't long before Wild Edna became Hurricane Nell, who in turn grew a foot in height and became Giant Susan, the Girl Bandit. The women were outlets for his illness. Some months Ned could barely breathe and then his heroines became opera singers. When he grew weak they would dance in halls before senators and, once, before the dazzled president. When he grew strong they grew weak and became imperiled damsels rescued from moustaschioed villains by a pale boy from New York.

At twenty Ned began to send his stories to the Philadelphia story papers. By then he had read in the newspapers of Calamity Jane, her comings and goings across the countryside. Every woman bandit, lady sheriff and melting sweetheart in his imagination fused into one and was named after Jane. His stories sold so well and were so popular with readers that Ned Wheeler and Calamity Jane were married in the press without ever meeting each other. Stories in the papers of her real adventures became tinged with something he was proud to call a Wheeler-esqueness. She was now the Heroine of the Hills, embroiled in scandal for her reckless love of Deadwood Dick, the Black Prince of the Road. Artists sketched her for the cards that came with chewing tobacco. Perhaps she found herself there once or twice, unraveling the packages.

Ned's stories attracted the attention of two New York publishers, the canny Mr. Erastus Beadle and Mr. Robert Adams. Mr. Beadle and his assistant Mr. Fox visited Ned one day with a plan. Mr. Fox was a small man in a black bowler hat. He stood a bit behind Mr. Beadle, his head barely reaching the other man's shoulder. He stepped quickly back and forth, one foot to another, in obvious excitement. Mr. Beadle was as tall as Lincoln with a long slender nose and deep-set eyes. His voice, when he spoke, was soft and persuasive.

Mr. Wheeler, said Mr. Beadle, we have an idea for a new form of reading material. I believe it will be popular.

We'll call it the dime novel, piped Fox, although we could sell it sometimes for a nickel. Yes, said Beadle with wide smile, it will be a kind of booklet, released weekly, with an illustration of your story on the cover. I believe that millions of people will read your work, sir, now that millions can read. Millions of people, men and women from New York State to Santa Fe, will come to know your Calamity Jane and love her deeply, as you so obviously do.

That night Ned's mother visited for dinner. As she peered into the stew on the stove, counting out the pieces of beef and carrots and onions, he told her about Fox and Beadle. She lifted her face, wet with steam, and crowed and stamped her feet.

Oh, Ned, she said, I have always loved your stories, especially the ones with Fearless Frank!

Mama, calm down. It's only new. Who knows what printed stories will do?

Oh, Ned, she said. She grabbed his face and kissed him. I don't care. I've felt so many times that you were writing yourself back to life!

Martha

|||||||||||||||||||||||||||||||||||||||||

SHE VISITED HER BROTHER, ELIJAH, IN A HOLDING cell before he was transferred to the penitentiary in Wyoming to serve five years for trying to defraud the railroad. He had forced stolen cattle onto the tracks to be killed and then filed claims for their replacement.

The guard was polite, asking after her day as he brought her to Elijah's cell and offered her a wooden stool. The jail was a wheelless wooden boxcar attached to the sheriff's office. The room was long and narrow. The doors on either end of the cart were left open to facilitate some breeze. It was September, hot still, and the mad colors of the trees, gold, pink and red, were visible through those doors. The room contained three small cells divided from one another by bars. It was a set of cages like the ones she had seen in traveling circuses.

Elijah was in the middle cage. He pulled himself over on a stool and gripped the bars. She sat and looked at her little brother. He was shaved bald. His skull was lumpy and his forehead cut and bruised. He had gained a lot of muscle and he looked just like their father, with his same rounded shoulders and thick neck. All the fat had melted from Elijah's face and his features were stark, almost brutal.

There was hardly any trace of the soft sweet hammy boy. He shook his head and reached through the bars to cuff her ear.

It's a nice place, she said.

Oh, thank you.

They play music?

They fiddle for me.

What do they feed you here?

Oh, pastries filled with warm apples and ham and bread, hot fresh bread, thick with butter, and yam soup with cream, and I drink whisky every night to fall asleep.

Well then, you eat better than ever. You look like someone danced on your face.

He covered his eyes with a thick hand. Don't say that.

The light through one tiny window shone narrow rays on the bucket that still held his shit and piss. Flies gathered there and on a tray with a little empty bowl, and on the pillow that lay at the head of a cot so narrow she knew he must sleep on his side.

I'm all right. You look like someone replaced my sister with my brother.

She laughed and slapped her knee. Her brother's nose was obviously broken and his eyelids were misshapen.

They beatin' on you?

Don't look at me. Look at you. What would Mama say?

She could smell the vinegar of old sweat on his clothes. His teeth were big and yellow from nicotine. But his smile was the same uncertain line.

She would say, The two of you get to sleep! Tomorrow we are going to a wonderful place where your father and I will be rich and you and your sisters and brothers will all stay together. A pony for every child!

Well, that's true. She was crazy hopeful right up until she died. Lena said you had a baby?

Martha nodded and sighed raggedly. I had a few. I don't have any now.

I'm sorry, Marthy.

It's all right. I had a stepdaughter, Jesse. She was Steer's daughter. I tried to do well by her. I tried to get her into school. I took her to Deadwood with me and introduced her all around as mine and they held a big benefit to raise the money to send her. And everyone was happy and drinking and cheering and congratulating me. When they handed me the money I was so overcome I offered to buy them all drinks and I spent it all, thanking them.

Elijah laughed sharply. The guard looked over.

Steer beat me, she said. He stabbed me and he hit me in the head with a rock. I hollered at him and I hit back. But I left before he killed me. I left Jesse with him. He wouldn't hurt her. She was his.

Don't cry, Marthy. I'm sorry, Marthy. I should have been with you.

No. You're my little brother. I should have been watching you.

No one could watch me. I always was bad.

No, stop it. You never were bad. You did some stupid things. So, you like insurance fraud?

It don't like me.

Can I do anything for you?

No. You need to leave me behind, he said. He snorted and wiped at his nose with his sleeve. She remembered this action.

When we were little do you remember how I was always catching rattlesnakes with my hands? he said.

Yes. I remember them wrapped around your arms.

And you said, Fuck you, Elijah, let them go. You never understood I couldn't let go—once I had them I had to cut their heads off or they would turn on me.

You could have let them go by throwing them.

I cooked them up in soup with yams and we all ate it.

That's right, we did. They were delicious. You did a real good job feeding us. Elijah, remember when we were scouts together?

Yes, I showed you how to be a boy. We watched the war together and we never gave away her secrets.

Remember skating on the river?

In our army boots.

Can you be good, Elijah, when you get out of here?

I tell you, Martha, I won't get myself hung, but there is no reason for me to be good.

She studied him in silence. Their faces were level. You look so hard, she said.

He blinked and his chin quivered. I'm not hard, Marthy. I'm not good but I'm not hard.

I know, Elijah. You won't get yourself hung. You'll go to Heaven on a whirlwind. You're my little captain. You're our pony boy. Remember Annie on your back?

He nodded, his chin tucked up tight to his collar. I'm glad they didn't live to see us, he mumbled. I'm glad they didn't live to end up this poor.

Shh, I'll tell your fortune. Guard, she called.

The guard looked over from the doorway. She saw him in silhouette against the sunlight. He was a skinny, disinterested man, wearing a too-large uniform.

Please, can you bring us water and a cloth so I can tell my brother's fortune?

The guard was at the end of his shift. He knew who she was and he was pleased to eavesdrop for a story to tell. He had no sense of anything bad that could happen so he brought her a shallow painted basin filled with water and a little cloth.

Come nice and close, Elijah, she said.

He pushed his face against the bars. She brought the wet cloth to his eyes and wiped away the dirt and dried blood. She lifted his eyebrow with her thumb to see a cut on his eyelid.

They really hurt you. Move your head back a bit so I can reach all of your face. Kneel here in front of me and give me your hands.

He knelt and she held his hands, turning them over and over and wiping at the lines and in between his fingers. She soaked his fingertips to loosen the grime and used her longest nail to clean beneath his. She kissed his knuckles and put her forehead in his palms.

Take off your shoes and give me your feet, she said.

He sat down and pried off his shoes and tore his socks from his wounded feet. She washed her brother's gnarled toes, the bony outcrop of a bunion and red ragged sores on his ankles. When she was finished the water in the basin was black. She stirred the dirty water with her finger and leaned over, studying the mud and how it settled.

What does the water say? Elijah asked.

It says you are good. You were always a good brother and I love you and you should always call on me if you need me.

Miette

||||||||||||||||||||||||||||||||||||||||||

MY HOSTS, JOHN AND SARAH, WERE HONEST AS eggs and they agreed that Calamity Jane had been reported last in Virginia City so I decided to change my route and go through Montana first. In the morning John helped me to pore over maps of the trails and plan my way. Sarah fried me eggs and bid me well, packing me bread and water for my journey. My clothes had been washed. My body was warm and clean after a long bath. I had a big bag of fresh deer jerky. The deerskin I had fleshed and hung for the night and rubbed with salt. I had more bags of salt to take with me. My horse was brushed and fed. The sky seemed like a lovely bright dome such as you might find over a Christmas scene in an ornament.

WE PASSED through a great netherlands of hoodoos, under the chins of giant scouts. The air was so full of ghosts I could hear them. The stone path, uneven beneath my horse's feet, made me feel as if the earth was rocking. We meandered all day over the body of the landscape, around concretions that might be shoulders and ribs and knees of a sleeping being. Echoes dissolved into whispers. We stopped to drink from Milk River and I saw carvings in the stone side of a steep butte, of battles between men with shields. I saw the bodies fall before me again. I saw a rider on a horse, long flowing lines of his headdress behind him and a buffalo before him. It put me off balance, I don't know why, but I was out of time with myself. Something heavy shifted in me.

It was raining when we crossed the border at Sweetgrass and saw the Turkey Track, the narrow-gauge railroad between Lethbridge and the Great Falls. What a strange crossing. The bighorn sheep stared at me like they recognized an idiot.

Looking at my maps I saw the paper was so wet the words were leaking.

Thunder rolled in with the evening from the northwest. The winds seemed warm. My father always said that the winds from the northwest blow warm. I knew that I must find a river. I determined to try at dawn because it was only at dawn and at dusk that I was sure which direction I faced.

I stood in the dark in the rain with my mouth open trying to drink. I filled my satchels with water caught in a circle of tin cans. I knew my horse had been thirsty all day so I watered her first. I felt I might die of thirst even while I drank. What, I wondered, is wrong with me?

TEN MORE days passed like this. Rain slowed, stopped, commenced and continued. In the brief breaks the air filled with loud clouds of mosquitos. On about the eleventh day I stalked and killed a long-tailed grouse to eat. I watched it for so long I almost couldn't kill it, but I was hungry and sick of deer jerky. I plucked it and cooked it in a pan over the fire. Having heard its neck break I had no nerve for slaughtering it properly. When it started to smoke I removed it from the fire and I bit into its breast and gagged until all the air came out of me. It tasted like dirt-bird dragged in poison. I had been too hurried to get all the damn feathers off and the fire took too long to burn deep and hot so the bird was half cooked with charred spiky feathers. I threw it on the ground and stomped on its smelly body, swearing and hating myself.

On the thirteenth or the thirtieth or the three hundredth day we passed through a forest of dead timber to some sort of dividing ridge where clean waters ran thick and white over the rocks. I remembered that all the rivers flow either to the Arctic Ocean, Hudson's Bay or the Gulf of Mexico. I wondered to where the Bow flows. My God, I was happy to see those beautiful spotty brown trout flip over each other in the shallows. I would have traded my clothes for a fresh brown trout fried in butter, but my clothes weren't worth a minnow's lunch. I washed and swam in the water and drank and splashed. I let my horse rest for an hour while I napped in the sweetgrass. When I woke I saw the brown body of a dead mouse beside me. I closed my eyes and I could feel myself shrinking. My father arrived beside me and crouched down.

Shall we bury it? he asked.

Yes. Will it go to Heaven?

Take my hand. Look at me. It's just a mouse, Miette.

HOURS LATER, close to night, which barely touches down in summer, we descended into the great canal of a coulee so deep that when I looked up from the bottom I saw the raised sides of the riverbed, the sediment stripes of purple, red, tan and black, and the way they towered all around me; it looked like I was surrounded by mountains, mountains eroding underground. We walked along a dry, braided channel made treacherous with ancient debris. Sinkholes gaped at intervals along the path. We passed protruding tongues of solidified lava. A sparrowhawk floated, looking for the little sweet meats cheeping in holes scattered across the walls. My horse stepped gingerly around rattlesnakes. As we rose out of the valley I saw a band of wild horses, watching us. A shaggy brown and white mare and her foal stood apart from two larger, smooth-coated gray horses.

A fort stood on the east side of the trail. It was a rectangular stockade of cottonwood logs with elevated blockhouses on two corners and over the main entrance. The main door was gone, leaving a broad gaping hole in the front wall. The other walls had been partly disassembled and some of the logs were chopped and piled near a large firepit. The burnt ends of dessicated wood lay crumbled in the center of a large black circle in the grass and dirt; streaks on the ground traced the absence of long flames.

Hey, I cried, hey out there. The valley behind me threw my voice back.

A figure appeared in the doorway. The sun was shining directly in my eyes and I could not make out if it was a man or a woman.

Come here, the figure said, come here.

I stilled my horse.

Come here. I want to see you.

I dismounted and walked slowly towards the voice.

Come here; let me look at you. Oh yes, it's you. You are the one I have been waiting for!

Who are you?

The voice laughed. Well, I am Calamity.

I stopped walking and blinked and squinted, trying to squeeze the sun out of my eyes so I could see her.

Come here. Come here, she said. She held out her arms to me. Her bony fingers moved like feelers in the air. She was small and her face was wrinkled and sunburnt. Her little eyes scanned my face. She gestured at the sky and I glanced at the white sun. When I looked back, her features were blacked out. She trembled and the smell of alcohol was strong on her breath. She smiled. Her naked gums were brown from nicotine.

At last. I'm so glad you're here.

Who do you think I am?

I have been praying for you to come. Follow me.

I walked behind her, watching her narrow body. She muttered to herself as she teetered along.

We circled the fort to a hole in the ground. It was the mouth of an abandoned well. A thick rope was tied to a fence post nearby and the length of the rope fell down the well.

Go, go down there, she said, pointing. Her arms and legs were shaking as if she would collapse or dance.

I looked down the well. No. Why do you want me to go down the well?

You have to. You have to. It's a dry well. It's not so far. There's gold down there, a box of gold, and bones, the bones of all my children. Go down and get the gold and get me the bones so I can bury them properly. I will pay you. I will pay you in gold to bring me the bones. I need them. I need to bury my children.

I'm sorry but I have to go.

Spittle gathered on her chin. She shook her head. My children are down there, she cried. You have to help me get them up.

No.

You have to! She clutched her head and wept and gasped.

IN CALAMITY'S WAKE

73

I waited for you! I prayed and I waited for you to come and help me. You can't leave me here alone. Don't you see how dark it is down the well? They were only children. If I can just give them a decent burial. I—Oh please help me. I need for them to go to Heaven. I don't care about myself. I only need my sweet children to be safe in Heaven. They are your sisters and brothers on this earth. You must see how wrong it is for their little bones to stay hidden in a well.

How did they get in the well?

I put them there! She turned and stomped in a circle. Goddamit, should I have let the animals feed on them? Should I have abandoned them? I was young and strong and I climbed down into the well with each dead one held against me one last time, as if they were sleeping. I let them slip down and I promised I would come back and get them when the war was over. I promised them that I would bury them and mark their graves and they would go to Heaven.

What's your other name?

What?

You called yourself Calamity when I rode up. What is your whole name?

I don't know. I don't have no other name. I'm just Calamity.

Who named you?

The troopers. I followed them and they gave me a name. Get down in that well. Get down there and bring me my babies! Get down in the well! Get down in the well!

I edged towards the well and got down on my knees and peered down the endless cylindrical dark. I took a match from my pocket and lit it and let it fall. I took a stone and dropped it too and listened. There was nothing.

Please. P-please, she stuttered. It's not so deep. The well is dry. I would never spoil nobody's water. My children are down there. I need to bury my children. I will give you all the gold but what I need to bury them. Please, please. I need my children.

I tested the rope and it held. There were knots tied every few feet and I used these like the rungs of a ladder as I climbed down. The sides of the well were slimy beneath my hands. I felt around and held on with my other arm. Finding nothing I descended deeper.

There's a ledge, she called. Feel for the ledge. That's where the gold is. It's all wedged in a big hole there, halfway down. Have you felt it yet?

No.

I ran my open hand around the wall, rotating on the rope. I slid down another few feet and tried again. I could see nothing. A few more feet and a few more.

There's nothing here, I called.

Can you see the bottom? Can you see the bones?

No. There is nothing here. It's the wrong well.

Nothing? No bones? No skulls? No bag of gold?

No, nothing. I'm coming up.

The rope burnt my palms as I pulled myself up. At the top I climbed out and faced her. She was livid, stomping in the dirt.

I see with perfect clarity, she shrieked, what you have done. You stole my babies. You stole their sweet little bones and the money I hid to pay for their burials.

Tears mapped her cheeks.

No, I said.

Yes! she shrieked. You have robbed me! You have robbed me!

I did not. I looked. The well is deep. I do not even know if it is dry, but there are no shelves, no places money could be hid. You said you were young; if the bodies were ever there I don't think I could find them now.

I raised my hands in a gesture of peace and between my fingers I saw the little black O of a gun muzzle shaking at the end of her arm. Her whole being was aiming itself at me through the mouth of that gun. I thought of the little gun tucked in my belt but I could not bring myself to draw on her.

I swear I have not robbed you. I looked hard. There's nothing in the well, I said. It's not the right well!

I heard a clap and I looked at the ground and watched the grass and stones get sucked back into the earth as I reached up to hold my ear.

You shot me, I said as I fell.

Martha

‖‖‖‖‖‖‖‖‖‖‖‖‖‖‖‖‖‖‖‖‖‖‖‖‖‖‖‖‖‖‖‖‖‖‖

THESE ARE THE KILLED (BY BILL): DAVIS TUTT, A good friend; Bill Mulvey, tried to sneak up on Bill; Samuel Strawhun, a foolish cowboy causing a disturbance in a saloon; John Lyle, a disorderly soldier of the 7th U.S. Cavalry Regiment; Phil Coe, a saloon owner with whom he had an ongoing dispute; Special Deputy Marshal Mike Williams, by mistake when the man rushed to Bill's aid. Also, Indians, a number debated depending on the politics of the day.

THESE ARE the killed (by the international shooting sensation, Calamity Jane!): No one.

Miette

|||||||||||||||||||||||||||||||||||||||||||||

I WOKE FACE DOWN WITH MY MOUTH FULL OF DIRT and blood. The pain in my ear was so great it was almost beyond feeling. I lifted my hand to touch my wound and I could not be sure if the raggedness dried into my hair was complete or if I had lost the ear. It was perfectly dark, perfectly silent. I dragged myself to a sitting position.

My horse, seeing me rise, walked over to me and touched my head with her muzzle. I rubbed her face and held her to help myself rise. I was weak and bleary-eyed.

Together we stumbled towards the fort thinking to sleep in shelter until sunrise. Near the entrance was a burnt-out firepit with wood piled beside it. I set a fire and peeled off my bloody clothes. I used water from my canteen to try and clean the wound but the pain was such sharpness I could not force my hand to finish. I did not want to stand long, naked in the firelight, so I pulled the black dress from my pack and drew it on.

As I dressed I felt so bitter, I conjured and twisted that beloved voice.

Make her pay, daughter, for all of the years that she put you out of her mind.

Why don't you turn around? another voice said behind me.

I spun and saw the Hag standing there. Did you follow me? I asked.

She nodded. She was dressed in trousers and a man's shirt and a hat, all the fabric dusty and falling apart. The clothes must have belonged to another of her long-ago guests.

What do you want from me?

She smiled and stepped forward.

Go away, I said. You turn back and don't follow me. I don't care that you knew him.

I loved him, she said.

No. I loved him. I loved him so much and that's why I came here, because he asked me to go to her.

I know that, she said.

For a moment I thought I could see through her.

Go away, I said.

But a lot has happened. He didn't know what he was asking of you.

I shook my head and began to pull her dress off my body. It caught on my ear as I yanked it over my head and I screamed. I heard it rip. I threw it at her and she caught it. We stood looking at each other until I covered my eyes with my fists, leaning the heels of my hands on the cliffs of my eye sockets. After a few seconds of brilliant stars I lowered my hands and turned to my horse and swung my body up into the saddle and we rode away from her as fast as we could.

After twenty minutes, forty minutes, whenever it was that it started hurting to run, we stopped. I looked behind me to make sure she wasn't there. The crickets were silent. The dark was thinning and although the moon was low I could see through the trees of the forest. The trees lined up as if receding bands of soldiers stood at attention and between those slim lines I saw the body of a wolf stepping so smoothly it might have been bicycling. I stopped and stared. The black creature also stopped and held my gaze, thinking. My heart about to explode, I stirred my horse to trot away.

Martha

|||||||||||||||||||||||||||||||||||||||||||||

S HE WAS BORN FOR THE FOURTH TIME IN MONTANA at the confluence of three rivers. It was May 1859. Around the world, society was at its height. Gounod's *Faust* was being performed in Paris. Whistler was painting *At the Piano.* A French tightrope walker, Charles Blondin, was walking across Niagara Falls on a tightrope. Dickens and Darwin were writing their masterpieces. The Baseball Club in Washington was being organized and the steamroller had just been invented.

But her birth went uncelebrated.

Her mother's name was Mollie Bliss Connoray. There were complications and Mollie died in childbirth. Her father's name was John Connoray and he died in a thunderstorm riding for help for his struggling wife. So the baby came into the world and within the hour was completely alone. By the time someone found Mollie Bliss's body, the infant had been spirited away. She was never found but all around the cabin were the broad footprints of wolves as well as pointed scat containing bone fragments and Mollie's hair. It was assumed the girl was eaten. No search was made. But in 1865 a boy living in the area claimed to have seen a naked girl with hair down to her knees fishing with her hands in the river. She was, he said, tanned and quick. She grabbed the fish and threw them behind her onto the dirt where they flapped together, sending teardrops of mud into the air. Later someone claimed to have seen a girl in the company of wolves attacking a herd of goats. For years similar stories accumulated, until footprints were found with pawprints and a hunt was organized.

On the third day of the hunt the girl was cornered in a canyon. A gray wolf stood in front of her snarling and bristling until it was shot dead. The girl collapsed and cried over the body of the wolf, rocking and holding the head of the beast to her breast. When the hunters approached she growled and barked and as they grabbed her she bit and tore their flesh with her teeth. One hunter cracked her head with the butt of his gun and she fell down unconscious. They bound her and took her to a nearby ranch and locked her in a room. When she woke she howled and howled and howled until the men were on their knees with hands over their ears.

That evening a large number of wolves, apparently attracted by her incessant mournful howls, came to the ranch. The cows and horses and all the domestic beasts on the ranch panicked. The men shot into the dark, killing their own livestock as well as the wolves. In the battle she escaped.

Several years later a surveying team reported a teenaged girl playing with two wolf pups on a sandbar. After that she was never seen again as the wolf girl.

She emerged in Deadwood as Jane, who had learned hunting from the wolves and how to travel great distances between territories without supplies. She forgave the men who tried to rescue her but she longed for her wolf family, most of whom had been killed that terrible night. She drank until the human words left her mind and then she howled.

Miette

||||||||||||||||||||||||||||||||||||||||||||||

I WOKE WITH MY EAR SCREAMING HOT AND IN TERRI-
ble pain. I was naked, asleep on the back of my horse,
who stood drinking from a river. The Hag was gone. The
awful woman who had shot me and who was not my mother
was gone. My skin was stained from sweat and blood that
had soaked the black dress; there were dark gray rings
around my wrists like cuffs. I took my normal clothes from
my pack and walked into the river with them, letting the
water do what it could. I waded out into the chill, turning
and rubbing until I was restored to my original color. I
wrung out my clothes and hung them over the branches of a
nearby tree to dry. I fed my horse and held onto her for
warmth, embracing her until the steam off her skin
reminded me to take the deerskin from my pack, which I
did and wrapped myself in. I fell on the ground and shook.

The sun rose and dried my clothes. I saw patches of the
purest blue between the clouds. The wind made its shapes
over me and a few hours later I got on my horse and began
riding through a dictionary of pain.

AIR IN ear.
Air, bubble in left ear.

Air, coming out of ear, alternate currents of cold and
warm.
Air, forced into ear on blowing nose.
Alive in ear, something is.
Animals burrowing in ear.
Animals, crying in ear.
Artery, large, throbbing behind ear.
Balls, circulating in ear.
Band, or cord, drawn tightly from ear to ear.
Battery of gunshots discharged in ear.
Beating, on an iron bar, tremulous tingling in ear.
Bells, ringing in the distance.
Bird wings fluttering momentarily in ear.
Biting of electric sparks on ear.
Blood bursting out of earlobes.
Blowing, into ear, someone was.
Boring of worms in canal of the ear.
Breath came from ears instead of lungs.
Cannonading.
Cat spitting in ear.
Coals glowing in small spots on ear.
Coldness in ear with numbness extending to
cheeks and lips.
Crackling of straw on motion of jaws.
Crawling, out of ear.
Creaking like turning of wooden screw in ear.
Crying of animals in ear.
Detonating in ears.
Digging in ear with blunt piece of wood.
Echoes in ear.
Forcing, of brain through skull out of ear.

Heat, streaming out of ear.

Hissing, of boiling water.

Ice, thin crackling.

Insects.

Instruments.

Jumping of fleas off of ear.

Kettledrums.

Knife, dull, pressing.

Landslide.

Locomotive.

Murmuring.

Noise.

Opening and closing in right ear like a fluttering.

Opening, in right ear through which air could penetrate.

Parchment drawn over ear on which I was lying.

Rain in ear.

Rain, striking ground beside ears.

Reports, of distant guns in ears.

Roaring, in ears like draft through a stove.

Roaring, like a partridge drumming.

Roaring, of storm in a forest.

Roaring, of waterfall.

Rolled back and forth shaking head.

Running, from ears, ice-cold water.

Running, out of right ear, hot water.

Rushing in ear of a stream of blood.

Rushing, through small hole in ear.

Rushing, of escaping steam.

Seashell in left ear.

Snapping.

Sound, a strange voice.

Sound, of bats.

Sound, of bells.

Sound, of clock striking.

Sound, my voice, like someone else's voice speaking.

Sound, walking at night, I hear someone.

Straighten out lobe of ear.

Teakettle beginning to boil.

Teakettle, singing.

Thread drawn through ear.

Thunder rumbling.

Twittering, of young mice.

Wax flowing from ear.

Windstorm.

Wood, stacking it for fire.

Worms, crawling under ears.

You singing.

Zither of nerve endings played by a demon.

Martha

||||||||||||||||||||||||||||||||||||||||||||||

I N C A I R O S H E S A W T H E G R E A T M I S S I S S I P P I L I T
up by the fires of an execution. She sat on her horse on the
bank watching as a Negro woman, the owner of a gambling
saloon on an old wharf-boat moored to the levee of the town,
was threatened from the bank by a group of twenty figures
bearing torches. Torchlight falling on the faces of the vigilantes drew long shadows from their eyes to their jaws, making them look ghoulish.

Calamity called to a boy in raggy trousers running towards
the crowd: Boy, what happened? What's happening?

The boy turned, jogging backwards, to answer her. They're
goin' to lynch her, he said. She bin winnin' all their money.

Calamity rode her horse around to get a better look at the
scene. The crowd grew as more and more people ran to the
wharf with sticks and torches and rifles. Soon it was a hundred strong and fire heated the air. On the wharf-boat the
thin Negro woman in a gray dress stood, yelling back at her
would-be killers, Get away from here. You too stupid to keep
your money! Get away from here! The Lord won't forgive you
people if you shed my blood! You all going to Hell like
demons! You gonna burn! You gonna burn, not me. Get away
from here!

The vigilantes began to move into small boats and they rowed over. Soon the black lines of rifle stocks were like spokes surrounding the woman on the wharf-boat. Someone gave a signal, though Calamity didn't see or hear it, and the boat was set afire and cut adrift. As it floated out into the current, the woman on the bow fell to her knees screaming and crying and covering her eyes with her hands. After a minute she got to her feet and went into the cabin. The vigilantes were calling to each other, We got her now! We got her! Where is she? Can you see her?

When the wharf-boat was well into the stream the woman appeared standing at the freight opening. Her hair was wild, released from its severe bun, her eyes were wide and her whole body tensed. She rolled a large keg of powder into the middle of the open space. She stood in the light of her burning craft, with a cocked musket in her arms, the muzzle plunged into the keg of powder.

I dare you, she screamed, I dare you to come on and take me! You demons from the underworld, you white Satans, you whoremongers, you come and get me!

The night was soaked in silence. The small boats kept at a proper distance now, their occupants floating, stunned. The flames licked up the sides of the wharf-boat, growing thicker and brighter until enormous sheets of flame cradled the boat. The woman stood, floating down into the darkness that swallowed the river, with her cocked musket still in the keg of powder. She cursed and defied her executioners. Calamity rode to the water, swung off her horse and waded in. She swam, limbs thrashing in the water, towards the woman.

Jump, she yelled. I won't let them lynch you. Jump and swim away from the boat. She screamed at the vigilantes, Put your guns down. Put your guns down. She's a woman. Are you going to burn her alive? Are you gonna hang a woman? Put your guns down. Goddammit, put your guns down!

Calamity heard an explosion. It was a boom that struck her in the gut; she felt it move through her. She saw the wharf-boat sink. Sparks showered the water, fell on her wet hair.

Damn you! she screamed. Damn you! Damn you! Damn you! She smacked and punched and kicked the water as she waded back to shore.

There was a long silence from the people in the boats. Their arms were at their sides, weapons on the ground. Their expressions were astonished. A number finally spoke out in sincere voices as if to a jury:

She didn't have to do that.

I didn't have the heart to lynch a woman nigger.

We would have taken her in for cheatin', that's all. We were only trying to frighten her.

Nigger woman was crazy.

She had a death wish.

Don't they all.

Miette

||||||||||||||||||||||||||||||||||||||||||||||||

S O, YOU ARE ALIVE. THAT'S GOOD NEWS! I must have passed out from the pain, while my horse found the trail and kept us moving, for when I heard that voice, my eye was on her neck and my arms were numb. I called, Whoa, and she stood still.

The voice belonged to a cheery little man mounted on a giant horse, a black mountain of a horse with a white heart on its chest and a white mane and tail. The man's moustache was equally oversized, hiding all of his lower face but the fraction of a lip and a small bit of chin.

He smiled at me and chuckled. I thought you were dead! he said.

Not yet.

Well you were headed in the right direction.

For Virginia City?

No, you are headed the opposite direction of Virginia City. You were headed in the right direction for death, riding around unconscious.

I looked around me. The trail looked the same ahead as behind.

Are you sure I'm going the wrong way? I said. Every word

sent pain shooting across my scalp. My arms and legs felt stuffed with sawdust.

Yup, I just came from visiting my sister at Alder Gulch. You need a doctor to look at that ear, he said, moving his horse in and leaning down to peer at my head. He whistled through missing teeth. You need some help or you are gonna lose that head, he said. If you don't mind Indians I have some friends nearby who could fix you up better than any misfit money-hungry doctor.

I looked at him. His brow was crinkled with such concern it was comical. His horse and my horse assessed each other, waiting for an answer.

Yes, I said.

WE FOLLOWED him towards an encampment. I struggled to stay conscious through the pain. He called the Indians Blackfeet and when I corrected him, struggling to say Blackfoot, he said, Oh, you are a Canadian!

I stopped talking. It wasn't that he was saying anything wrong but opening my mouth to answer the man was enough to make me want to murder myself.

I could smell my wound and I felt a warm sticky flow down my neck. As we passed a rock formation he waved and I saw an Indian girl on horseback. From her expression I knew I must look mostly dead. She led us to a big campsite. There were twenty rings of teepees in large open clusters between two coulees. Five cairns were arranged along small hills at the north end of the camp. There were Cree and a few Assiniboine and some from other tribes there, but this was the Blackfoot reservation. She exchanged a few words with my rescuer and then with my horse and then she caught me as I fell from my saddle.

With the help of some friends she brought me to her family. I looked up at their faces as they carried me. I had never seen such beautiful eyes.

I lapsed into unconsciousness again and when I woke I lay within a circle of women in a large teepee. They had wrapped me tightly in blankets, soaked my hair with water, mopped the blood from my head, neck and shoulder, and tied a poultice to the wound.

Apos-ipoca, one woman said and made the sign for dry-root.

I lay on my back on the soft earth and turned my head to watch an old woman laying out a sheet and then spreading bright beads of saskatoon berries across it to dry.

How's that? someone asked me.

Thank you.

A WOMAN and her daughter tended to me, clucking at the look of my ear. They called me sister-in-law. I didn't know why. Still, it was full of kindness. I knew by the movement of their voices that I had lost my hearing on the wounded side. The hours were different in length depending on the level of my pain. The painful hours were like tacks in my brain and the smoky minutes spread out over everything. I sucked on chokecherry mash and bit the inside of my cheek when they checked my ear. I told them about the woman at the well, about my father and how he had sent me to find my mother.

That was not her, one woman signed. That woman is crazy since the war.

Yes, said the old man, whose name was Theophilus Little. That poor woman is one of the common casualties of the war.

She lost everything but the conviction that her children are still out there somewhere.

WHEN WE were alone Theophilus smoked a pipe and did not speak much, although he laughed often at his own thoughts. His laugh was a rumble from the chest, almost like pleurisy. I slept and slept, waking most often when my head was being gently examined or my body shifted into a seated position so that delicious stew could be pushed through my lips.

As the days passed, the pain in my head grew noisy and hot; I hated even to move my neck. But when I lay perfectly still, I listened to the language of the people around me. It brought me back to Zita. Theophilus called the mother Lizzy and the daughter Poesa. Children and other adults came and went, clearly asking after me. Outside I heard grandmothers singing to babies and the horses gaily neighing. Lizzy and Poesa spoke some English and I some Blackfoot but mostly we communicated by signs.

Pain? signed Poesa.

More, I signed.

Poesa bid me to lie down and she spoke to her friends for some minutes.

While they spoke I stared at the interior of the cone of the ceiling. My head expanded and contracted around the drum of my bloody heartbeart.

IN THE night I woke shaking, the uncontrollable movements of my body adding to my pain. Poesa was there, watching me. She fed me and wet my face, wiped at the eternal sweat. She swaddled me tightly in blankets against my weak protests and fanned me with my hat. She sang me back to sleep as if I were her own sister.

I woke in the dark and she was there, asleep at first and then woken by me. She lifted my bandage and clucked when I gasped.

Pain bad, she said.

I nodded. I hurt too much to speak or sign.

She nodded and then she pulled up her clothes to show me a scar in the center of her belly, another navel, made by a De-Creator.

I live, she signed. Your wound is not as bad as this.

How? I signed.

She shook her head.

Thank you for saving me, I signed.

She wiped my face and neck again. She lifted the packing and examined my wound carefully while I clenched my teeth. She poured water into the wound and then packed it again with agrimony.

The fever is good.

Is my horse here?

Your horse is good. She is outside waiting for you.

She sat back and watched me burn. I saw her there through drifting eyelids whenever pain pushed me up to the surface of consciousness.

THEOPHILUS STAYED on, sleeping in a tent he erected outside of the teepee. He came often to sit with me after the draining and washing and packing of my wound was done. He sat on his pack with his knees far apart and his elbows rested on them. His limbs were skinny as sticks inside his worn clothes but his feet were either bizarrely long and thin or else he wore shoes stuffed with newspaper.

Will you go on if the infection heals?

If it heals?

I'm sorry. I believe that it will continue to heal. Poesa says that it will and she knows her patients.

She's very kind.

How do you feel?

Less dead. If I don't move or breathe then not so bad. When she pulls the stuffing out of my head I feel like murdering myself.

Theophilus nodded. He leaned in close to sniff my head and whistled sympathetically.

Will you go on looking for your mother?

Yes. If I can I will.

After a long pause he asked, Why do you want to find her?

I don't. Or, I don't know. I promised I would.

A broken promise made to a dead man is seldom punished.

I had no answer to that and so I was silent. Theophilus cleared his throat a few times and rolled his eyes and rocked on his heels and swapped his cup from one hand to the other and back.

I love these people here, he said. Lizzy and her husband took me in one winter. I didn't know nothing about Indians. They showed me a buffalo jump where the bones of the buffalo have been layered over thousands of years. Around the fire they told me about the dog days, the days before horses, and the winters of starvation. They made me feel like part of a human family.

That's good, I said.

If you are who you say you are, I knew your daddy. That is, if you can trust Jane when she says that it was Bill.

I tried to sit up and cried out with pain. I held the packing against my ear and breathed hard through my teeth until I could speak.

How do you know him?

He's dead; you don't have to worry about finding Wild Bill. Is that who it is?

I don't know. That's what she told my father.

He looked confused. She couldna told Bill; he was dead before you were born.

No. I meant the man who adopted me.

Oh, well. That makes sense. I knew Wild Bill in Abilene when he was city marshal and I was selling lumber. He was a good man. I never knew anyone so sorry for killing a friend.

For killing a friend?

Yup. Say what you will, he was a gentleman of the old style in a savage new land.

I turned my head to listen better and Theophilus took this as encouragement to tell the tale he had been holding for me.

I WAS there ahead of the rush, got there in the winter, what year was it? 1881, 1882? Anyhow, in the early spring great herds of Texas cattle arrived to be shipped to the eastern markets, thousands upon thousands. The air smelled of manure and every conversation was held against great mooing. And with all those cows came cowboys, cattle owners, cattle buyers, gamblers, thieves, thugs, murderers, the painted women, the rich, the poor. Ha, talk about the Wild and Woolly West; everything calm went wild, everything went woolly.

I had a lumberyard on Texas Street near Walnut Street. The streets were always full, jammed full of saloons, gambling dens, dens of infamy of all kinds of character, cut-throats, robbers, murderers. There was money being passed from one end of the street to the other and back up again all day long. I'm not exaggerating, I have not half told it. It was indescribable, it was the wickedest place on earth, and I was there on Texas selling lumber.

Every cowboy, black, white, or Hispanic, that came into town had to pass my office door. There were hundreds of them every day and every son of a gun had two guns, each as long as an Ohio fence-rail. These boys came to town to drink and gamble, get rip-roaring crazy drunk, try the patience of the whores, and towards evening jump on their ponies and shoot hundreds of shots at the sky.

Wild Bill was our city marshal. He was much admired. He was born in the state of New York, his father a Presbyterian deacon, but, as he told it to me, he grew up leaning west. I just went west and just couldn't stop going, he told me.

He stood over six feet tall, straight and erect, graceful as a woman. He had superb fingers, shoulders like a Hercules.

Like a Hercules? I could not resist.

Yes, yes, your father was a handsome man. The women loved him. He had gold hair flowing to his shoulders, an eagle's eye and two big ivory-handled guns, loaded to the muzzle, always hanging on his belt. I tell you this not to win your favor. The bad men feared him. He never missed his mark when he fired those guns and the bad men fled from him as mice flee from a storm.

He killed someone?

Yes.

Who?

He killed Phil Coe. Oh, and a few others. He was not a violent man but you must understand it was hardly possible back then to get through your whole day not killing someone. Phil Coe ran the Bull's Head saloon. He was a vile character who for no reason I ever knew just hated Bill. Well, for some cause he vowed to secure Bill's death, marshal or no. Not having the courage to do it himself, but having many a drunk indebted to him, he filled two hundred cowboys with whisky one day, intending to get them into trouble with Wild Bill in his role as marshal, hoping that they would all get to shooting and in the bedlam Bill would get shot too. But Wild Bill learned of the scheme and cornered Coe, his two pistols drawn. Just as he pulled the triggers, a policeman rushed around the corner between the two men and the pistols and the shots from both guns entered that poor man's body, killing him instantly. Of course, Bill then shot Coe twice in the belly. And then, whirling around with his two guns drawn on the drunken crowd of cowboys, Bill said, And now do any of you fellows want the rest of these bullets? Not a word was uttered. Get on your ponies and ride to your camps or I'll shoot into you, Bill yelled.

A hush was upon these boys and in less than two minutes the mob had vanished into the darkness. Bill went back to the boy in the dust but he was already dead. Bill carried the policeman in his arms, like some sweetheart, to the coffin-maker and bought him a fine coffin. He paid all the expenses for the man's burial, including bringing his mother from Kansas to claim the remains. He felt real guilty about killing a man who surely was rushing to his aid.

My father killed two men?

Oh, he killed more than that! But things like that just happened all the time. Blame it on the moon, blame it on the stars or the whisky.

Blame it on the stars.

Or the whisky.

Well, thank you.

No never mind. Don't feel too bad about the killings. He got shot himself playing cards. Revenge killing, if that makes you feel any better.

It does not.

Martha

||||||||||||||||||||||||||||||||||||||||||||||

S HE BEGGED POKER ALICE TO READ HER THE REPORT
of Bill's death in The Special Correspondence of the
Chicago Inter Ocean.

A pistol was fired close to the back of the head, Alice
read. The bullet entered the base of the brain, a little to the
right of the center, passing through in a straight line, making its exit through the right cheek between the upper and
lower jawbones, loosening several of the molar teeth in its
passage, and carrying a portion of the cerebellum through
the wound.

Martha gagged hard and fell forward. Alice caught her by
the shoulders and pushed her back in the chair, holding her
as long as she could. Alice won three four-hour games with
Martha crying on her, soaking the lace at the neck of her
dress, until the men said they wouldn't play; they couldn't
bluff over her weeping.

Most mornings she could be found sleeping in the mud
under a wagon. She had a little plot of land but she let it lie
fallow. Bill was in the ground. Plagues took over. Locusts and
beetles churned the plant matter. Nothing could reach
through the grief; she just drank and drank and drank and
drank and drank.

Bill's death was the beginning of hard times in Deadwood. Gold nuggets turned into frog bones, pans turned into colanders, piggy banks turned into rattles. The crowds that had flocked to the hills fled. Poker Alice couldn't get a game going. There were days and days when the only things said out loud were *sorry* and *goodbye.* Everyone said they were coming back, just going home to take care of something quick and planning to return. For a while Alice kept promises to watch belongings, keep an eye on families. Eventually all the families were sent for but not the belongings, and so she treated those as hers, an inheritance of dead hopes.

Those that stayed did so because they didn't have anywhere to go and they were getting richer. Women left in the town had more dresses than dancers, more pots and kettles than a big hotel, shoes for every occasion. The whores at Mollie Johnson's collected twenty-seven cats, ten dogs, five horses and nine canaries. They lined the canary cages with shredded claims.

On winter nights under skies bent with stars, Poker Alice, Martha and Dora DuFran went riding in abandoned carriages. They tore up and down the empty streets under the falling snow whooping loud at the wind. They stopped at every bar and had a drink and got back in and raced up and down the main drag again. When Alice, Martha and Dora laughed at once it was like the sun coming up.

Miette

|||||||||||||||||||||||||||||||||||||||||||

THERE ARE POINTS WHERE TIME ACCORDIONS. IT IS as if the past, the present and the future are pressed together in a concertina, every minute touching, and then every minute open to be viewed. It was like that while I lay there in the pointed dark of the teepee at night, with the warm bodies of Lizzy and Poesa sleeping beside me. Often I dreamed of my father, and then I would wake to recall the past.

In dreams he lifted me from my boots and we rose in the sky in a great balloon, my horse beside us. The balloon carried us over oceans churning with dolphins, whales and giant turtles. Together we crossed purple mountain ranges and white deserts, the sand braided and ropy, moving with the wind as if alive. My horse nuzzled my neck and breathed in my ear. I held my father's hand and I could feel the specific weight and the shape of his fingers. I inhaled the smell of him and it was warm and edged with soap.

And then I woke and he was gone. The dark was so complete it hurt to try to see so I closed my eyes and covered them with my hand.

Father—

JOSEPH, WHY come here?

Forgive me, Father.

Come in.

I busied myself with the dishes in the hot water while my father steered one of the mission priests to the main room. I peeked around the corner. The old man was in his robes but the dust from the ride had reached his waist. A sunburnt circle of skin showed beneath the thin dark hair on the crown of his skull. His neck was creased over the collar. I had seen him before but not in our house. He was from the mission closest to us. He rode a pinto around in the afternoons and stopped to talk to the children. I remember his tanned neck squeezed by the white collar.

Come in.

I won't until you tell me.

Tell you what? Tell you what?

Until you tell me that you will take my confession. I have come to repent. You must take my confession.

I will, of course. Come in. Come in and sit down.

My father arranged the chairs and the screen. I stood quietly by the sink. The rooms baked with August heat. The father rushed in and knelt on the floor not bothering with the screen or any pretense of privacy. My father put his hands on the man's shoulders in compassion and then drew a chair into the middle of the room and sat with his back to the man.

Please, turn the chair. I don't want to hide from you or from God anymore.

My father turned his chair around and sat, legs crossed, hands folded at his knee.

In the name of the Father, and of the Son, and of the Holy Spirit. My last confession was two days ago.

My father recited: Jesus said, I am the good shepherd. The good shepherd giveth his life for his sheep. Say the sins you remember. Start with the sin you find most difficult to say. After confessing all the sins you remember since your last good confession, you may conclude by saying, I am sorry for these and all the sins of my past life.

O my God, I am heartily sorry for having offended you and I detest all my sins, because I dread the loss of Heaven and the pains of Hell.

Say them. Say the sins you remember. Ask me for help. Ask God for forgiveness.

Help me; I have abused my authority. I have a lover.

You committed to be celibate.

I have broken that commitment. I have been with an Indian girl. I have been with her many times. I am sorry for this sin. I am sorry too for riding to the mission in the south and confessing there.

Why do you confess confessing?

Until this day I rode to share confession with a priest who does the same as me. I came to you today to make a real penance. I need forgiveness. I hurt this girl.

What do you mean, you hurt the girl?

I hurt her by taking her trust, Father. I feel real affection for her. I would never injure her, but I hurt her family and the trust they gave me. I hurt myself, Father. I abused myself when I could no longer bring myself to abuse her. I betrayed my vows. I betrayed God. Father, I come to you to ask for punishment. I must have forgiveness.

There was a long silence that I did not understand and then my father said, Our acts have grave consequences but forgiveness does not depend on penance. When you ask God for forgiveness you are forgiven. Listen to the words of absolution, the sacramental forgiveness of the Church. Make the sign of the cross with me. God has already forgiven you. It is not to me or to God that you must atone now. It is not inside the Church that you must seek forgiveness. Apologize to her. Apologize to her family. Make it right with her and them. Leave the Church and give thanks to God for your freedom. Give thanks for his mercy which endures forever. But leave the Church. Brother, be who you are. Be with the girl if she will have you, if that is what she wants. Otherwise go home to your family. Brother, you are no longer a priest. You are only a man. Look me in the eyes. You don't have to be a good man but don't be a fool; don't be a liar and keep on pretending.

SHH.

I opened my eyes and Grandmother leaned over me. Her face was as evenly dark as the room surrounding us. She left me and moved to adjust a smoke-flap. She returned to me and by the thin light filtering in, her moving hands were visible.

You were fighting in your sleep, she signed.

With who? I signed.

With God. You were fighting with God's eyes.

Martha

||||||||||||||||||||||||||||||||||||||||||||||

EYES ARE BEAUTIFUL, SHE SAID. EVERYONE HAS beautiful eyes.

Miette

||||||||||||||||||||||||||||||||||||||||||||||||

O N T H E L A S T D A Y O F M Y R E C O V E R Y A H A P P Y L I T T L E
boy brought me a small trunk painted brightly with beau-
tiful forms. Inside was a blanket and food. I thanked him and
shook his small hand and hitched the trunk behind my saddle.
I set out with Poesa and four young riders to get back to my
journey. There was the most astonishing difference between
the morning and the afternoon. In the morning it was cool and
windy but in the space of four hours we experienced a wonderful wonderful transition back to summer. I was near insensible
with the heartless blue sky. My friends had fun with me, making jokes with each other as if I wouldn't notice. They moved
like angels, joints all made of butter, and they had high smooth
voices. I enjoyed just listening and following and watching the
world as it changed. They left me at the Bozeman Trail. It was a
sadder leaving than I had expected.

We rode on. My horse snorted frequently to remind me
that I was not alone. We rode over hills and through ravines.
On the top of a high hill we stopped. A great Indian burial
ground was spread out before us. There were some thirty
large coffins and seven small coffins. Around the coffins
were the artifacts of domestic life: spoons, hair combs,
copper nails, leather belts, shoes, beads, books. Most of the

coffins were closed but some were open and empty. Several had broken lids and the bodies that lay inside were bleached by sun and rain, wrapped in blankets and skins. One hand bore rings and the arm of another skeleton was ringed with bracelets. Wildflowers grew between the coffins in abundance, flowing over the hill as far as I could see. It was quiet and as clean and clear a day as I had ever known.

We traveled on and, some hours in, weakness overcame my ambition. I felt a pain in my ankle. I steered us to the river and let her drink while I rested. Removing my boot I saw a huge black boil.

Who-oo, I whistled at the hard swelling. When did you arrive?

I fell back in the grass feeling as if I was made of infection. Full of fevers of every kind and my thoughts breaking apart. The little river beside us was about ninety yards wide with bright rapids. Staring at it cooled me. Fish were jumping or getting tossed into the air over the slick rocks. The beds of the streams were formed of smooth pebbles and fine gravel. I rolled to the edge and sank my foot into the water, which was perfectly transparent when I stared down at my boil. While my boil cooled I looked around. It seemed deep enough in the river proper that you might be able to canoe for quite a ways. I sat there for hours. At times I saw deer drinking at the opposite bank and ducks paddling by.

I measured the likelihood that I'd have the energy to build a lean-to to give me a bit of shelter and maybe to stay the night here. The evening was beautiful, the sky a brilliant red. The mosquitos and the gnats were suddenly thick with the dusk but come night the wind would blow them all away.

Dear Boil, I asked, should we go on from here or stay

where there is water, fish, firewood and no annoying crazy people?

Well (I answered in the voice of Boil), you can stay a little longer with your boots off to let me breathe.

Dear Boil, does the soft gravel in the beds of all these streams come from the mountains?

Yes, said Boil, I think it must because it is the same color and likely stones just keep falling and falling down the steep sides of rock smashing and smashing until they splash into the river and break down into tinier and tinier pieces rolling all the way to the river's end.

Dear Boil, I asked, is that thunder or did a tree fall?

Well, said Boil, it could be a tree unless we hear it again.

Dear Boil, if there was lightning would we be safer in our hut or on our horse?

Well, said Boil, I don't know but the water helps the lightning so let us not go swimming.

Hours passed before I heard thunder. The thunder swallowed and I saw lightning divide the air overhead and then great big balls of rain fell hard upon me from what still seemed like a clear sky. My horse whinnied and blowed and snorted. I put together a lean-to as quickly as I could and and pulled on warmer layers, mostly just to keep them dry. The raindrops hitting the water exploded as if they fell from the sky only to be shot by some invisible marksman. My poor horse, outside, was tense in the sudden squall. I watched her, thinking, I hope she does not get rain scald. If she does it will take weeks to heal and no more riding every day.

Boil, I said, this is bad news.

I half considered if it was a smart or a stupid idea to build a little fire inside my hut, measuring in my head how high the flames might reach, how close to the branches that made up my walls, how smoky it could get and what stinging my eyes might be able to take before I would be driven out. I half considered getting on my horse and riding as fast as we could in whatever direction looked clearest. But she was already so wet and if I rode her too long without letting her dry it would cut her skin to ribbons.

One time, Boil, I began, when I was ten or eleven, a horse that was dark like mine ran into the town along the trail at daybreak. My father and I were in Rosebud to get supplies and sell some eggs. It was winter so daybreak was almost noon. I watched the horse run down Main Street so fast it looked as if its front legs were going to buckle, as if it would roll head over hooves and break its long neck. It was the horse of the butcher, who had just been shot by his wife on the doorstep of the barbershop for twisting and breaking his son's arm. The horse pulled free of the rails by the trough where he was tied while his master had a shave. He ran into the town and out the other side and through the cemetery and at the end of the cemetery he fell, hooked by a prairie dog burrow. He broke his leg. And the woman who, dry-eyed, had shot her husband dead came weeping down Main Street until she fell on her knees in the cemetery and shot his horse.

My horse rolled an eye at me and pulled sharply against the rope that tethered her to a tree.

Come here, come here, I called to her. Get in here. And I pushed her as far into my makeshift hut as she would go and I stood for the rest of the storm outside in my hat, which became a birdbath, with a stinking muddy mat and the deer-skin wrapped around me.

Rain became shooting stars long after midnight. I lit a fire and smoked my clothes by it. She came out of my hut.

Hello, I said. How are you feeling?

She turned her head.

What do you think? I posed to her. Say you had a mother and by all accounts she was a liquor-loving wild whore. And say that in her wisdom, knowing herself, she gave you to a good man and in her wisdom she never contacted you, never wrote to ask how tall you were or if you were still alive. And say the one who had mounted her was a killer and he was dead before he ever knew about you. And say your real father, the man who was both mother and father to you, who made you a safe home and loved you—in his wisdom as he died when you could say nothing but yes to him—set you on a journey to find the woman who chose not to be your mother. Should you follow her wisdom and leave her be? Or should you follow his wisdom and find her and force yourself upon her?

The night was replete with silences: the silent sky with all its silent stars, the silent ground, the silent birds and insects. My horse was most silent of all. I wished on one star to find my mother and on another to give up.

We have to go on, I said. We can't give up.

I sipped cold muddy coffee from a recovered cup. Soon after that I fell asleep.

Martha

‖‖‖‖‖‖‖‖‖‖‖‖‖‖‖‖‖‖‖‖‖‖‖‖‖‖‖‖‖‖‖‖‖‖‖‖‖‖

H EAR THIS. I CAN'T FREEZE TO DEATH NOR CAN I
drown. I tried poison but it only nourished me.

Miette

||||||||||||||||||||||||||||||||||||||||||||

I WOKE TO FIND MY HORSE GONE, MY SHELTER COL-
lapsed and the wolf settled down to sleep at my feet. My
heart tried to leave my chest. She was easily six and a half feet
long and half as tall. Her muzzle was long and tapered. Her ears
flicked in her sleep as did her giant feet as if she were dreaming
of running down an animal. I lay still and tried to breathe quietly and recall what I knew about wolves and whether any of it
would save me.

Wolves don't get hungry. They are always hungry. They go
without food for days, sometimes weeks, and then gorge on
meat until they are drunk. I turned my head to look around
me for pieces of my horse and saw none. I listened to the
deep breathing of the wolf and watched her sides rise and
fall. I could smell the damp hay of her fur and a duskiness
that penetrated me with shapeless emotion. Her tail twitched
and I tried to imagine ways to creep away.

A long time ago there were ten million buffalo and enormous herds of antelope and deer on the Plains. Giant grizzly
bears and plains wolves feasted and lived very well. But white
men came and all the animals began to disappear in great
numbers. Zita had told me about wolves and their hunger.
She had told me that if you copied wolves closely enough you

became a wolf. There were once two white buffalo hunters who tried to copy Indian hunters. They draped wolfskins over their backs and crept up on a herd of buffalo. The Indians knew to become wolves to hunt but the white hunters did not understand. They did not know that the Indians became wolves and that when they did this, they would be different, merciless. The two hunters were pretending to be Indians pretending to be wolves. Under the skins they moved inside the circle of buffalo, feeling such a gnawing in their bellies. Their desire to kill was greater than their desire to live, and once they began to kill they could not stop. They needed a signal that would not come. They shot until their guns got hot and were in danger of exploding in their hands. But the herd of beasts remained placid. They stood like great trees in a dense forest as if all this were happening on some other plane of existence. The hunters dropped animal after animal. The sight of blood and the bellowing of the wounded did nothing to rouse the herd. They stood, oblivious, solid, benign, until a gust of wind changed direction and suddenly the sight of so many carcasses materialized, and they stampeded. The two men stood mesmerized by the bodies that lay before them. At the sight of their success the blood hunger instantly abated and shame flooded the marrow in their frail human limbs.

I shifted and tried ever so slowly to stand. She opened her eyes, looked at me with irises like honey in the sunlight and stretched her long limbs, flexing the full span of her broad feet. She yawned and I heard her voice squeak and saw the truth of her teeth set in the hard pink gums. I felt the breeze as she shook her head and stood and looked me over and turned and padded away, looking back a few times as if she expected me to follow her. When at last I turned around I saw the long yellow carcass of a cougar with an opened throat lying in its own blood behind me.

I WEPT and wept over my horse. The physical pain of that grief startled me, the way it ran down my arms and legs, the way it tightened and flexed and heated and chilled inside me. Around me the signs in the landscape seemed to unravel as if I were looking at a map in a dream with nothing written on it. I was afraid to move for fear I would step farther away from real people. But I was more afraid, I was most afraid, of disappointing my father.

As THE night came on I observed the time and the distance of the sun and moon's nearest limbs. I found myself making lists, reducing everything in me and around me to lists just to force myself to stay with the present, keep sane, keep hold of my thoughts, which were slippery in my loneliness.

MEASURED THE width of the river from the point across to the point of view. Measured the curve of the flow around the rocks. Measured how white the foam is on the banks. Measured the height and width of reeds. Measured the length of time I need. Measured my grief at losing my horse. Measured her body with my memory. Measured the hours passed measuring. Measured the likelihood of wolves. Measured the length of the grass in the shade and in the sun. Measured the shadows from clouds. Measured the undertow based on daisyheads thrown into the water and when they are pulled under the surface. Measured the reasons for continuing. Measured the wound on my head. Measured how much I love my father.

Measured how much I still hate her. Measured the limbs of the sun overhead. Measured the shimmers of heat in the air. Measured the motes of pollen. Measured the missing stirrups. Measured the horn of my lost saddle. Measured the supplies uneaten. Measured the guilt I might feel. Measured the relief from completion. Measured how much I can believe anyone. Measured how long I have been away. Measured the cascading water. Measured the space between stars. Measured how sticky the cottonweed. Measured the smell of clover and columbine. Measured the days I spent reading the Bible. Measured the number of things I remember. Measured the length of his black robe. Measured how small he was after death. Measured the drops of water administered. Measured the rise of the moon. Measured the loudness of my stomach growling. Measured the comets. Measured the streaks of color. Measured the shock from watching the spirals. Measured the collapse of the universe. Measured the nut of fear in my chest. Measured the strength of my tearducts. Measured the maps unopened, unread. Measured the depths of my resignation.

I BUILT a fire and found a good knife in my pack under the collapsed lean-to and I hacked away at the warm skin of the cougar, and then at the meat on the shoulders. I was awkward and the cuts were ragged. Memories of Blackfoot hunters offered only weak guidance to my hands. By the time I finished my hands and arms felt bruised. But the cooked cougar meat was sweet and rich like some deeper angrier venison.

I stared into the fire feeling my eyeballs shrink and dry and my skin heat. Sweat sprung up on my lip and neck. I closed my eyes and saw the afterimage of the flames. When

I opened my eyes night had fallen and the Hag was sitting across from me, her gaunt face illuminated.

She cocked her head and stared at me. She sat like a dog, squatting with her backside suspended just over the ground, her arms straight, hands between her feet, braced. Her small eyes glistened over her cheekbones, one of which looked flat as if it had been broken at some point and healed. She wore the black dress, which was torn and ragged so that one white shoulder and her upper arm were exposed. Her feet were bare and filthy. I felt contempt.

What do you want? I asked her.

Every morning I woke up waiting for him. I had fantasies about him coming back for me. It must have been like that for you too. You must have dreamt of your mother returning to embrace you, to wash your face with kisses, promising to never leave you again. Didn't you?

Sometimes, I said. I looked at the moon and the stars that were nestled in its halo.

Nights around here are filled with ghosts, she said. As soon as it gets dark they come out of the ground. The streets of all the little towns are teeming with spirits on parade. There are hordes of spirits, all the longing, unforgiven souls, wandering in purgatory. There are too many ghosts even to pray for. And because we cannot pray for them we are reminded of our own sins and errors. I begged your father to marry me. I said, The bishop will pardon us, release us from shame. He said, I can't be released from shame. I told him, I can't live without you. He said, Then live alone. I tried to tell him that life had herded us together. It was not our fault. We had to find each other because we were the two loneliest people on Earth. We were the same and so we had to be together. He pushed me into a chair and he broke my door when he left.

She sat across the fire from me with her head lowered, flexing her feet and rolling her hands in the dirt. Her white hair fell forward, obscuring her face. She moaned softly, persistently, until the low sound became almost musical. She rolled her head back and forth and rocked on her heels.

I tell you this so that you know I understand, she said. I understand what it is to be rejected. I understand what it is to spend years imagining someone's return.

I tasted salt on my lips and realized that tears were pouring out of my eyes.

I scratched my nails in the dirt, grabbed a rock and threw it at her, not to hurt her but because I did not believe she could be real. The rock hit her shoulder and rolled down the length of her arm into her hand. She squeezed it and looked at me. She tossed the stone back to me and I caught it.

If you want to throw stones at someone you can throw them at me, she said softly. She stood up; the skirt of the dress was torn off at the knee and I saw the thin bones of her shins shining under her pale skin. Then she stepped around the fire until she was almost at my side. She moved back a few paces so that there were five or six feet between us.

Throw the stone.

I squeezed it and then I threw it. I winged it at her face with all my strength. She ducked and smiled. She leaned over and picked up another stone and tossed it to me.

Again. I aimed the second stone at her eye, which suddenly seemed brilliant and yellow over her cheek. She turned her head and it flew past her lips. She tossed me another stone. I yelled when I threw the third stone, some unintelligible accusation. It grazed her temple but left no mark. She didn't even wince. Then I was scrabbling in the dirt, grabbing and throwing stones and handfuls of sod and grass and animal hair and she was weaving and spinning. She was whirling, ecstatic at the precipice of another world I could not see. I couldn't hit her. I heard my own voice grow louder, echoing in the darkness. I heard myself screaming, Why did you leave me? Why did you leave me?

Suddenly I was tired. My echo faded in the distance. We were face to face, each in our loneliness. Suddenly she stood still.

I like you, she said. Good luck. I hope you reach her in time.

A fine line of bright blood ran down her forehead.

I'm sorry, I said, shocked that I had hit her. There was a shudder of a small earthquake beneath my feet and a human-sounding rumble and then it was daylight again. The ground where she stood was empty.

It was not quite dawn when I woke and began to walk. My feet clove the sandy earth. My hat had begun to smell and so I tied it upside down on my head with some twine to let the sun bake out the soggy bell of it. An intermittent breeze shook the tree branches overhead loosing sprays of dew. Birds shook their wings. As the clouds retreated, rising higher in the sky and becoming white, the sun lit up the new spaces of blue. I stared up imagining red kites with tails that whipped behind. I could feel the burning tug of the cord on my finger. My father laughing, tucked his robes into his pants so that he could run with me. The wind in my ears.

OH, FATHER, I love you. I could hardly hear your laugh but I could see your lovely teeth. You told me once that to be a good priest, to be a man of God, to do God's work, did not require simply the ability to love but the ability to fall in love endlessly with every person, with humanity.

Let out more string.

It's pulling on me.

It's very high. Let's run.

We ran in the long grass; the dandelions stained my legs and the cuffs of his trousers; the kite and I tugged at each other. When we stopped running we stood side by side breathing fast. My father put a finger beneath his collar to wipe away sweat. I scrunched up my eyes because the sun was so compelling. My arm was stretched out long. The kite waited in the sky. A hawk veered to avoid us.

I'll help you study your Latin after dinner.

Can I grind chocolate for dessert?

There's no more chocolate, but there is some honey-comb. I have letters to write. We had best be on our way. Zita is waiting.

Father, I love you, I said.

God loves you, he said touching my hair as if it might break.

ZITA AND my father understood each other's silences. He steered me to her and she showed me warmth in ways his propriety could not allow. It was Zita who lifted me from my boots and held me when I wept. It was Zita who sang to me when I raged against my outcast state. It was Zita who rubbed my arms and legs when I was sick.

This was before the Indian Act forbade the Indians to

leave the reservation without a pass. There were so many children then. They were like herds of deer running up and down and around the coulees and sloping hills. So many children were adopted into families within the reserve it seemed as if there were twenty for every adult. My father reminded me of this often. He told me too that tens of thousands of children across the States were adopted every year. He tried to make me see myself as less alone.

Mighty Miette, he said. So many parts of being who we are start as fictions about belonging. You belong, as much as anyone.

But the children on the reserve were not like me. They had lost parents and siblings and even whole families to illness and war. But they were kept in, whereas I had been pushed out. I watched them play and I wanted to join them. They called to me and gestured invitations but I couldn't move my legs. I watched them pump their arms and run with wide smooth steps and fall and roll and get up and jump and run some more and I just couldn't move my legs.

We lived on the border of the reservation. He said this was respect; if we lived on one side or the other we would do so as spies. Truthfully, I think that he did not want to be watched by either side. He was as solitary as he could be and still perform his duties. But if he rejected other clergy, he welcomed the Blackfoot to visit us in our little shack.

Zita helped us to bake bread and make soup to deliver to the poorest homesteaders. The poorest were also the oldest, as if life had been sucked out of them with their wealth.

One evening when I was inconsolable over being forced into some promise of better behavior, Zita held me and rocked me. She hummed and sang and I smelled her warm skin, the tan and the berry and the clean water of her arms. I squeezed her hand and followed the veins of her arm with my finger. I felt love opening like cherry blossoms along the branches of my nervous system. Life drawn so sweet.

Zita, I said, why do I have to keep my promises?

Zita, who was great as a snowy hill, cuddled me and said, Shh, you keep your promises because you are a good girl. I'll tell you a story about a bad girl. This is the story of a bad girl and a wonderful bird.

There was a young girl who, one day, was walking about among the trees, collecting berries and being happy in the summer heat. She saw something that seemed very strange to her. A little bird, all blue and red, was sitting on the branch of a pine tree. The bird danced back and forth on the branch. Every little while it would make a strange noise, like a whistle, and every time it made this noise its eyes flew out of its head and fastened on a branch of the tree. Then the bird made another sort of noise, like an inhalation, and its eyes flew back to its head. The young girl called out to the bird, Brother, teach me how to do that!

The bird considered her. If I show you how, the bird answered, you must not send your eyes out of your head more than four times in a day. No matter how much you want to see something you must keep this promise to me. If you break your promise and send your eyes out more than four times, you will be sorry.

Brother, whatever you say I will do. It shall be exactly as you say, Little Brother. It is for you to give, and I will listen to what you say.

The young girl knew to respect the bird and she was pleased by his generosity so she intended to keep her promise. The bird taught her how to send her eyes out and she was so excited that she did it four times immediately. She danced back and forth with pleasure. The bird's gift allowed her to see around trees and watch the bear fishing with its cub. She was able to see over the forest, to follow the bald eagle in flight. She saw the cougar crouch to attack a doe. She saw the worms churn the earth underfoot. Why did that bird tell me to do this only four times? she lamented. He is only a bird; he has no sense. I will do it again. So once more she made her eyes go out, hoping to see the whole earth from the heavens, but now when she called to them they would not come back.

She shouted out to the bird, Brother, help me! Come here, and help me to get back my eyes!

The little bird did not answer; it had flown away. The young girl felt all over the branches of the tree, all over the ground, all over stones and bushes with her hands, but she could not find her eyes. She walked through the rivers letting the water stream between her fingers. She felt along the riverbed, the water filling her mouth and washing her face. But she could not find her eyes. So she went away and wandered over the prairie for a long time, weeping and calling to the animals to help her. Because she was blind, she could only rarely find something to eat, and she began to be very hungry. Her stomach roared and her limbs shook. A wolf came by and teased her, brushing up against her legs and pushing her forward with his nose and holding her hand in his wet mouth. The wolf found this teasing great fun. The wolf brought a piece of buffalo meat close to the young girl's face.

She said, I smell something dead. I wish I could find it. I am almost starved.

She felt all around for it, felt the wolf's head and neck. But he had already dropped the meat into the dirt and she could not find it. Finally, when the wolf was doing this, the young girl caught him, and said, Give me your eyes.

The wolf pulled away but he looked at her and when he saw her in pain with hunger he consented and the young girl plucked out one of the wolf's eyes. She put it in her own head. Then she could see and was able to find her own eyes, but never again could she do the trick the little bird had taught her.

Zita, I said.

Yes.

Can you stay with me? Can you stay all night?

No, little Miette. I have to sleep by my children.

THE NEXT day when Zita came she was so excited she chattered in a mixture of Siksika, English, French and hand gestures, trying to impress upon me the importance of a chief named Crowfoot and Treaty 7.

Crowfoot was the Blackfoot chief and her uncle, and he was spending time with her family.

Zita?

Yes, Miette.

Who are those men? I said, gesturing with my elbow towards the window.

Two men in black shirts and dirty pants with ragged hats and sweating dark faces walked towards our house carrying carbines. They walked slowly, with the guns raised and trained on us through the window. Zita grabbed my shoulder and pushed me into the pantry, shushing me as she closed the door. The smell of flour and sugar and dried herbs filled my nose and the dark filled my eyes. After a few minutes I could see shallow lines of light through the boards of the door but I could hear nothing of what was happening outside. I trembled and gulped shallow breaths. The men were dressed in furs and rags. I had seen men like them before and I knew they didn't like Indians. Once I overheard a fur trader in confession saying that he had spiked homemade liquor with strychnine to kill the Indians he traded with. Zita, I knew, would not hide from them.

I sat on the floor and wrapped my arms around my knees. We didn't have anything to give them. Around me were cans of beans and jars of chokecherry jam, pickled onions and carrots. My throat ached. I stood and carefully, quietly, opened the pantry door.

When I arrived at the window and peeked out, I saw the men with guns pointed at Zita and I saw my father standing between them with hands raised in apparent surrender. He fell to his knees and Zita stepped in front of him and held out her hands, palms up. I knew we had nothing to give them.

And then the sound of many hooves working the ground made me look beyond the terrible scene. Five Blackfoot warriors arrived and encircled the men, Zita and my father. They sat high on enormous, restless horses in saddles made of wood, sinew and bone. They were armed with guns uncannily similar to those toted by the white men. Their clothing was made of white buckskin and it reflected the sunlight. One man wore a necklace of claws. This man drew closer to Zita on his horse and they spoke together.

You should go, she said to the white men in a strong, calm voice. Leave your guns.

She turned to my father and offered him a hand to help him stand.

THAT NIGHT we sat with Crowfoot and the warriors outside around a fire that smoked heavily because the wood was green. As the moon rose Zita ushered me to bed and tucked me in.

They were going to rob us? I asked her at last.

Yes, she said, but they were seen.

Are we safe now?

Your father will keep you safe. I need to go back to my children. There will be trouble because of what happened today, she said. White men don't like Indians to fight back. Crowfoot protects us. He knows the white man's ways and he knows the white man's intentions. He met with the white men in the beginning, when they started talking about the reservations. The chief white man spread many one-dollar bills on the ground and he told Crowfoot, This is what the white man trades with; this is his buffalo robe. We trade with these pieces of paper.

The white chief laid all his money on the ground and it made a large circle. This was to show how much he would give if the Indians would sign a treaty.

Crowfoot took a handful of clay, made a ball and put it on the fire and cooked it. It did not crack. Then he said to the white man, Now put your money on the fire and see if it will last as long as the clay.

The white man said, No, my money will burn because it is made of paper.

Zita smiled and patted my chest under the blankets.

Crowfoot said, Oh, your money is not as good as our land. The wind will blow it away; the fire will burn it; water will rot it. Nothing will destroy our land. You don't make a very good trade.

But you wanted the treaty, I whispered. I wasn't sure I knew what she wanted.

Crowfoot was brave and he would fight but he wanted peace; he wanted to save our people. The buffalo were gone; we were starving. The white man had killed them to starve us but we could see that what had happened to the buffalo would happen to us. The old chief could see the future but he still had hope. Crowfoot said, we can fight them and they will kill us all. Or we can go onto the reservations. Our spirits will be dead but we will be alive and one day our spirits will come back.

Will the buffalo come back?

Yes. Sleep, she said. And then she left me. She left us.

And there was no one, no one at all to embrace me fully and rock me in their arms anymore.

Martha

||||||||||||||||||||||||||||||||||||||||

ARE YOU THERE? IS THIS WHAT YOU ARE looking for?

CALAMITY JANE!
THE FAMOUS WOMAN SCOUT OF THE WILD WEST!
HEROINE OF A THOUSAND THRILLING ADVENTURES!
THE TERROR OF EVILDOERS IN THE BLACK HILLS!
THE COMRADE OF BUFFALO BILL AND WILD BILL!
SEE THIS FAMOUS WOMAN AND HEAR HER GRAPHIC
DESCRIPTION OF HER DARING EXPLOITS!
A HOST OF OTHER ATTRACTIONS
THAT'S ALL—ONE DIME!—THAT'S ALL.

(One dime and I'm yours.)

Miette

‖‖

T HE ROAD AND THE TREES, EVEN THE CIRCLING
buzzards, and the clouds were all part of a panoramic
painting rolling around me as I walked in place in the center
of a cyclorama. I walked along the trail tracking the hours by
the sun that moved in a bright arc overhead. When at last I
came to a river I washed my face and neck and took off my
boots and socks and immersed my tender feet in the cool
waters. The boil was smaller but the balls of my feet were
alternately numb and painful. Stopping was a great relief.

It seemed like weeks since I had slipped into a warm bath
and scrubbed my skin clean and dressed in fresh clothes. I
chewed on some clover and rested. I had no sense of how far
the next house or town might be. I could build a lean-to and a
fire here and try my hand with a sharp stick at spearing one of
the fat brown fish swimming in the shallows at my feet. Little
bushes loaded with strawberries lined the shore. I reached a
few and ate them. They were sun-warmed and sweet. On the
opposite bank of the river I saw the crumbled remnants of an
abandoned firepit. Horse hooves had left a pattern of clefts
in the sandy earth along the bank. I sighed and dressed my
feet and went back to hiking towards the next haven or hole.

I stumbled along the trail until I came to a strange little

town called Star. It looked like it was picked up from some-place it made sense to have a town and then later, when dropped from the sky, it just didn't break. I did not really need to stop but I guess I was looking for someone to listen to. I followed a highly dressed woman inside the building. Her skirts swept all the dust from the floors. Her collar was buttoned almost to her forehead. I followed her so close she might have feared me but instead of running she led the way to the bar.

Now I had never had a drink of anything but wine and then only to take communion. So I truly did not know its effects. I knew that whisky drinkers sometimes beat their wives and horses and each other. I knew that hard liquor led to the Devil making women lose their minds and lie with strangers. I knew that sometimes you could die from drink-ing those liquids that burnt your nose from smelling them. But I did not know that anything bad could ever follow drink-ing wine. I wanted to be welcome and I wanted to say the right thing. I wanted to have a full glass and not one sip with a piece of bread that was His Body. I felt nostalgic, I felt greedy, I felt thirsty, I felt like I really wanted wine. So I stood at the bar.

The man behind the bar was also very well dressed. He was a big man with a big moustache curled tightly at each end. The woman drifted up the stairs and I never saw anything of her face but only the dark hair coiled at the back of her head, tucked in with a shell comb. It was like she didn't have a face with eyes and lips and teeth. But I had a face and I filled it with wine.

THE LAMPS stuttered, unable to hold the whole room in light. I closed my eyes and savored the heat in my cheeks.

Behind and around me I heard yelling and the crash of furniture. A wooden chair wheeled overhead in an awkward arc. But I was so warm and smiley and the pretty bottles were lined up nicely in the cabinets behind the man who filled my glass, which glistened when I laid my head on the bar. Someone started to speak to me. I thought it was only one man but frankly he might have been twins.

You're the one looking for Calam, he said. You look just like her.

Who are you?

He had round little glasses. They both did. And he wore a shirt that was so far gone I had no idea if it had seen better days. He had curly brown hair as long in the chops as it was on his forehead and a voice that sounded womanly.

Can I tell you something? they whispered. I hate the poor.

They leaned in to me so that I crossed my eyes and almost fell off my chair. I blinked; they made no sense.

I get nothing from the poor. They don't move me. They don't even entertain me. But your mother, she loved the poor. Oh, lady of enlightenment! Give me your wretched of the earth, your tired, your diseased, your alcoholic-no-good-lost souls. Give me every body, rejected and hated, lost and lonely—give me all of them. She is the real monument to humanity—your humanity, not mine.

After that, what they said about the poor got scary, like a crackle in your ears that hurts your mind. I shook my head.

How do you know my mother?

All my fault. I betrayed the only one who loved me. Prayers don't work. Prayers don't make the dying not die. Prayers don't make anyone lucky. Prayers don't stop an infection or seal up a bullet hole. Prayers don't bring on the rain or hold it back or make the ground good or the next man kinder than the one before. Prayers are just a way of telling yourself that all that extra thinking will come to something when there's no action left to take.

I don't know what you are talking about. How do you know my mother?

He threw back another shot and gestured to the bartender.

I fell over. He picked me up and put me in a chair and pulled the chair over to the bar.

You want some toast?

Toast?

It will take the edge off your drunk to have some food in your stomach.

No, thank you.

I was a doctor in Gomorrah.

Deadwood.

Joke. That's how I know your mother.

Did you treat my mother?

No, no. I knew her. She was a friend to everyone in town. When the smallpox epidemic came she volunteered. There were so many sick we set up a tent settlement outside of town. She sat the night shift with patients so I could sleep.

Do you know what it looks like? It's thousands of big hard fluid-filled blisters all over the face and limbs, in the mouth and throat; it's as if the body is boiling from the inside out. You can't even see the person's features anymore. They can't speak; even lying still they hurt. Sometimes they walk around with their arms held out from their bodies to ease their skin and I'd see their zombie shadows through the white tent walls when I walked up in the morning and it was still dark outside but the lamps in the tents rendered the walls practically transparent. The tents start to feel hot and close and the whole air stinks of illness and you know you are breathing it in over and over. I was there because I swore an oath but she was staying sober to help strangers.

How long could she stay sober?

I saw her do it once for six weeks. Calamity thought of how to protect herself and I thought she was crazy. She ate the scabs of a patient who had recovered. Later I read that the first written account of variolation describes a Buddhist nun practicing around AD 1022. That nun would grind scabs taken from a person infected with smallpox into a powder, and then blow it into the nostrils of a non-immune person. The cells in the scab are dead so the infection doesn't get passed on but the body produces antibodies. Christ, she was doubled over gagging from the taste, but she did it. Then when it was all over she drank her weight. I think she was trying to steril- ize her stomach.

Behind us a weird silence gathered. I turned and saw that the crowd of scrapping bullies had parted and they were stand- ing in a wide circle around a woman and a man. She paced in a tight pattern, her body braced, her head lowered, her gaze hard. Her face was bleeding. She had been hit in the eye and mouth. There was blood in her long pale hair. In her hand she held an unbelievably tiny gun. The man was fat. He held out his large hands to calm her. There was blood on the knuckles of one hand. She paced again and then walked to him and raised her arm and shot him between the eyes. The sound was like a frozen branch snapping. He fell backwards like a tree.

Ah shit, said the doctor. He put down his drink and

picked up a black doctor's bag from the floor. He went to the man, knelt at his side.

Go home, Trixie, he said to the woman.

He opened his bag and drew out a long metal probe from the mysteries within.

Leaning over the unconscious giant he inserted the probe into the hole and checked several narrow angles.

There's no brain here. He'll be fine, he said.

A strange music like wheels murmuring over rough terrain, or an idiot humming in a cemetery, broke through the human din. A man walked through the crowd playing the hurdy-gurdy and swung himself up on the little half-moon of a stage.

Ah-rum-ba-da-da-rrump-rrum-ba-da-darrhum-ba chanted the queer little violin-beast in his arms. He had a face that was round as a penny and dark as a burnt log. He wore a white silk hat, white vest and wool shirt with diamond studs and a straight-standing celluloid bon-ton collarette. On his high boots there were silver spurs and a red scarf hung from his belt, pulled through a poker ring.

Be not disturbed! Be not disturbed! he cried. This man who lies on the floor has been killed here every Friday for a month! Poor old Trimpy got to learn not to hit on Trix. Why she shot him in the eye just last week but not to worry, she ain't shot nothing else since then. She's as good as your own mother's angel, dear girl, dear, dear Trixie. Now, who, he said, gesturing dramatically to himself, is this man, so knobby and swell who stands before you? I am the Dutch Nigger Minstrel! First to record the old favorite "There'll Be a Hot Time in the Old Town Tonight," and one-time husband of the darling Mollie Johnson, Queen of the Blondes! I know, no one could believe it when I married the fairest white woman in Deadwood; my friends thought I'd never settle down! Not me, Lew Spencer! Blackest man outside of Africa, the proprietor of this dream palace and your host tonight in the resurrected Bella Union Theater! Tonight we have for you: myself!

The crowd laughed and applauded and stomped, sending small plumes of dust up from the floor to hang in the air and render the scene smoky under the gaslamps. As if cued by the dust, cigars appeared between the lips of half the audience, men and women alike. The smoke grew into halos around the heads of the patrons.

I know what you've heard but it ain't true—I only ever shot one of my wives and it still didn't keep the others from finding out I was triply married! Women are my weakness, and I'm hoping they are yours, because we have for you a human statuary made up of the most astounding array of beautiful ladies. We have a contortionist duo from Paris—Ontario, but still! We have Hottentots, clog-and-jig comic dancers, seriocomic singers and Ethiopian-Dutch-Irish comedians, acrobats, and double trapeze acts, sketch artists and some who'll perform feats of marksmanship, and the Deadwood brass band. Ladies and gentleman, this is a first-class vaudeville experience we offer! No burnt cork and tambourines! No half-drunk trollops in raggy pantaloons pretending to know ballet! What I offer you is entertainment without the ordinary vulgarities of show. I'll have you know New York has written us a letter full of envy! Stand back! Stand back because the awesome virtuoso that is none other than myself is here to open a show that will transport you!

Sing "Topsy"! yelled someone in the crowd.

Lew Spencer grimaced and shook his head and then

smiled. No sir, I have nothing but the newest, most illuminating music for you here tonight!

Sing "Topsy"!

"Topsy"!

Sing "Old Topsy"!

"Little Topsy"!

Lew Spencer bared his teeth. You are living in the last century, my friends. But for nostalgia's sake, and as I want your money, he sneered, I will sing to you that old favorite about the most soulless, most downtroddenest, most imaginary nigger that ever got set to music. But after this, dear people, I ask that you mature some and give my show your thoughtful attention.

Lew turned his back on the crowd, put down the hurdy-gurdy and did a quick softshoe with arms akimbo. Then he picked up the instrument and turned back to the masses, eyes glittering, a sharkish grin on his lips, and he spat out a vicious version of the old-time favorite.

Topsy neber was born,
Neber had a moder!
Specks I growed a nigger brat,
Just like any oder!
Whip me till the blood pours down
Ole Missus used to do it;
She said she'd cut my heart right out
But neber could get to it!
Got no heart; I don't believe,
Niggers do without 'em,
Neber heard of God or love,
So can't tell much about 'em!

This is Topsy's savage song!
Topsy cute and clever!
Hurrah then for the white man's right
Slavery forever!

I 'spects I'se very wicked,
That's jist what I am . . .
Only you jist give me chance,
Wont I rouse Ole Sam.
'Taint no use in being good
'Cos I'se BLACK you see,
I neber car'd for nothin yet,
And nothin cares for me;
Ha, ha, ha, Miss Feely's hand
Dun know how to grip me,
Neber likes to do no work
And wont without they whip me.

Don't you die, Miss Evy,
Else I go dead too,
I knows I'se wicked, but I'll try
To be all good to you;
You have taught me better things,
Tho' I'se nigger skin,
You have found poor Topsy's heart,
Spite of all its SIN!
Don't you die, Miss Evy dear,
Else I go dead too,
Tho's I'se black, I'se sure that God,
Will let me go with you!

This is Topsy's human song,
Under Love's endeavor,
Hurrah then for the white child's work.
Humanity forever!

Finishing, he threw back his head and cackled. Half the crowd looked appalled, threatened, while the other half cheered.

All right then, you happy fools! Drink my liquor and don't break my chairs! You're all sinners! he yelled, just as the pianola began to accompany the unfolding living statuary. Blondes, brunettes, redheads—women draped in transparent fabrics painted to emphasize the nipples and just barely covering the nether regions, drifted or rolled onto the stage and began assembling with their bodies some abstraction meant to convey a scene from classical literature.

LEW SPENCER relaxed at the bar beside me.

I know what you're thinking, he said to me in a friendly voice. Would this lovely man accept a drink from one such as me? I would.

The bartender laughed and poured Lew a long shot of golden liquor, which Lew then set upon his lower lip and sniffed before he drank it.

You'll like the food here if you're starving, Lew said. But if you're not I'd stick with the hoochinoo.

You were married? I said, for I could think of nothing better to say.

I am married, he laughed. Just don't know where any of my wives live now.

Who was the Queen of the Blondes?

Oh, Mollie. Mollie Johnson was a madam in Deadwood. I was performing at the real Bella Union and when she saw me she had to have me. But that was a long time ago. I know I look twenty-one, but it's all good living!

I'm looking for my mother; she spent time in Deadwood.

Long as you're not looking for your father! he laughed, and I knew by that laugh that it had been years since he had really thought anything was funny.

Maybe you met her; her name was Martha Canary—

—Calamity Jane! he finished my sentence. For the first time he relaxed and looked at me as if trying to see my features.

Calamity Jane, he said softly. He dropped his chin to his chest and the bartender filled his glass again. The statuary had dismantled itself and exited the stage and two men wearing only pants and suspenders were pretending to wrestle in order to demonstrate a bizarre range of motion.

Lew Spencer undid the cuff link at his wrist and folded back his sleeve to show the deep pits of smallpox scars. I looked at his face and saw tiny beads of sweat resting on thick makeup. He winked at me.

They wouldn't let me in the tents so she had to come to my bedroom, where I was hid, in Mollie's old cabin. She didn't care what anyone said. I can't even tell you what it means to have someone hold your hand and help you sit up and bring you water when you have been all alone expecting to die. It's ugly too, so ugly my wife wouldn't look, wouldn't come to see me in that cold shack. And it's dangerous, and Calamity didn't even know me except as someone that had chided her for being ugly. She was, he laughed falsely, a dirty-looking sow. And I was a foolish young man. I lived to be a bitter old man. But I lived.

I hope you find her. Tell her Lew Spencer is alive still. Tell her she can stay here for free as long as she wants, drinks and food on the house. Tell her that the woman who is better than her does not exist. None of my wives was half so kind, though they were all pretty.

I sat beside him collecting my thoughts, thinking about her caring for strangers but not caring for me.

You can stay here, if you need a place. You have a horse?

No. I lost my horse.

You're really her daughter?

Yes.

Do you need some help with something? Do you need a horse or train fare? Do you know where you are going?

No. Yes. I'm going to Virginia City.

She's not there. She was at the Pan-American Exposition two years ago and after that she roamed around a lot. But I know she's not in Virginia City. Your best bet is to go to Billings and see if Mollie Johnson has any idea. Or you can go straight to Deadwood and ask Dora DuFran. Excuse me; I have to perform.

He left me and leapt back up in front of the lights. A woman in a thin blue dress was wheeled onstage on a bed by a child who fled immediately to the wings. Lew knelt beside the bed and took her hand and crooned,

> Oh, why should the girl of my soul be in tears
> at a meeting of rapture like this?
> Oh, why should the girl of my soul be in tears
> at a meeting of rapture like this?
> When the gloom of the past and the sorrows of years
> have been paid by a moment of bliss.

In the morning I woke in a soft bed with the sun shining on my face. I came down from my room. The bar and the stage were empty, swept clean. The space was so clean that the brass rail around the bar glowed in the sunlight pouring in from the tall windows. There was a smell of wax and soapy water. From the kitchen came the smell of bacon frying. I sat down at one of the card tables and stared at the silent pianola.

Are you hungry? Lew asked, walking in from the kitchen with two plates of steaming eggs and glistening bacon.

Yes.

Yes. No. Yes. You don't talk much.

It was a wonderful show last night, I said as he put a plate down before me and sat across from me with his own. Without the makeup I could see his face was deeply scarred, as if someone had stabbed him with an awl a thousand times.

I'm glad you liked it. The trapeze act is hard in a space like this. He looked up at the vaulted ceiling where the two trapezes were tied to heavy beams.

I brought these for you, he said and he deposited three postcards on the table in front of me. On each was an image of a rough-looking woman.

Is that her? I said, feeling as if the wind had knocked me off a rooftop.

That's her big face, he said and laughed.

She does have a big face, I whispered.

I'm sorry I called her a sow, he said, I'm sorry I called her ugly. She wasn't ugly.

He sat across from me and ate without disturbing my racing thoughts. I felt weak. I felt he must hear my heart beating. After a while he got up and went into the kitchen and came back with two cups of coffee.

The first picture was labeled on the back *Martha Canary (Calamity Jane), Black Hills, 1875.* There was a stamp-shaped design in the upper right-hand corner.

Looking at her looking back at me from my hand I thought, this is where you put the stamp to send the postcard in which you tell someone that you saw her.

In the picture she leans on a large rock face, half lying down; the lichen on the stone shows up white in the photograph, as does the bright handkerchief around her neck. There is a skinny black tree bare of leaves beside her. It must have been fall. She looks straight at the camera, unsmiling but relaxed. She wears boots, trousers, a dark shirt with the cuffs rolled up and a brimmed hat. There is a mountain in the background and the furry outline of conifers. She would be somewhere between nineteen and twenty-three in this picture.

The second picture is labeled *The One and Original Calamity Jane, Miles City, Montana, 1880–1882.* It is an obvious studio shot. She sits, one arm on the top of a padded curved armchair, a plain band on her wedding finger. There is an Aztec design on the rug or the thick blanket over the back of the chair and under her arm. She is wearing a long dark dress with scalloped white cuffs peeking out from the conservative sleeves and a large white lace bib tied around her throat. The skirt is drawn into a bustle that peeks out from her hip and large bows of the same plain dark material run along the bustle-line. Her hair is ribbed with iron curls; a few tight ringlets lie on her forehead. There is a womanly hat, a stylish hat, on her head, decorated with bands of something that looks like tight little feathers. She looks stern or sad, stiff. She looks somewhat older than she could be but still very strong.

The third postcard is the most recent, from the Pan-American Exposition, 1901. She is dressed in full cowboy-on-exhibition beaded buckskin regalia, fancy gloves, a sharp, stiff hat. Her horse is beautiful; she has a white band down the middle of her sweet face. There is a lasso at the horse's shoulder and the design on her saddle blanket matches the design on Jane's suit. Jane holds the reins, arresting her horse. Much much thinner, in this photo almost drawn, she looks down at the photographer. There are white tents in the background. Her face is set in a deep, complicit frown.

I turned the postcards over and over again as I searched for some trace of me in her.

You can have them, he said. I bought them from her when she passed through. She was awfully down.

Thank you, I said. I did not speak again for minutes. When I did speak it was to shake myself free. Where did you learn to sing and dance and play like that? I asked him.

He stirred his coffee with his fork.

You want to hear my story? he said.

I nodded.

I'm like you, he said. I never knew my parents. They died of yellow jack when I was two. He straightened in his chair and put a hand to his chest, bowing his head.

Allow me to perform for you, he said.

Lew Spencer

|||||||||||||||||||||||||||||||||||||||||||||||

I ALWAYS HOPED THAT I WAS PART APACHE AND belonged here, or that I was something new, of Africa and America at once, a citizen of the world and not just the ungrateful ancestor of honest people stolen and dragged across the ocean to be slaves. Not just the son of two people who worked too hard their whole lives only to die in exile in their own excrement, for that's how you die of yellow fever. Forgive me this long recitation of my life, which I hope is in the Apache style.

We had a lot in common, your mother and I. But Calamity never wanted to perform. She did it to please people, to fill an obligation, to save herself from starvation. I grew up wanting to be a minstrel and see the world.

I lived with my grandmother in Washington, D.C. She was strict but I was her favorite person in the world. My grandmother took me to see the old Kunkels one Saturday when I was nine. She didn't like music that wasn't Church but she wanted to please me and I cannot convey the revelation that struck me seeing a troupe of colored folks on the stage performing, being in the center of everything. I was in awe of the banjo solo and resolved on the spot to be a Negro minstrel. Mr. Ford, in whose theater President Lincoln was assassinated, was the Kunkels' agent. My grandmother pointed him out to me as she told me about poor Mr. Lincoln, who she thought a hero. I got up out of my seat after the show and walked up to Mr. Ford and told him my ambitions. He laughed and introduced me to Mr. Kunkel who lit up a cigar and asked my age. I told them I was nine but very smart and eager to learn, and they promised, no doubt out of amusement or to escape me, to take me with them on a new traveling show when I was ready.

I did laundry and dishes at every establishment that would have me and I lay there in my cot at night making up songs in my head about heroes and ladies and thinking of circuses and shows. In the day I swept floors and brushed horses and every kind of work I could think of until my hands were raw and my arms were weak and then I bought a used banjo. I screwed pennies to the heels of my boots and I played and danced day and night until my grandmother began to fight with me and the neighbors in the boarding house complained but nothing could stop me. I practiced until my fingers bled and my toes went numb. I practiced until the landlord gave us a warning. And then I asked our preacher if I could practice in the church. He said no. I had to practice in the streets. The racket that I made at all hours and places can only be explained by youthful ambition, which is too broad to ever be contained by reality.

Well, the Kunkels never came back for me, and so, at the tender age of thirteen I ran away from home to find them. I traveled all over the Western lakes on the steamboats with my banjo, one suit that had belonged to my father and which I was never to grow into, and a wallet that ate what little money I put between its leather lips. I came pretty close to starving, but even after I gave up looking for the Kunkels I still dreamt of undertaking a barefoot tour of Europe and eating applause. I grieved for my dead parents and for my grandmother, who, I knew, would be broken by my absence. She had given me her waxing years and would need me when she waned. But I never returned and I never wrote. I evaded the House of Vagrancy and turned my coppers into a bankable sum by trading papers and books on the steamer *Northern Indiana*, commanded by the late Captain Pheatt. That old man threatened to throw me overboard every night when I clog-danced on the deck over his stateroom but he never disposed of me.

Once the steamer was laid up for the winter, I found a place to board in Toledo and argued a way to return to school. Of course that was when I ran into Ford and the Kunkels again and they again promised me that when I was ready they would take me with them. In the course of a month I abandoned everything to bring together a band of boys from school who all were failing chemistry. I formed with these boys a musical troupe with myself the appointed musical director.

Our instruments consisted of my banjo, three sets of bones, a tambourine, a bent triangle and a wheezy accordion. With this motley of soundmakers we set about making life miserable for everyone in the neighborhood. On certain evenings a mob of angry neighbors rushed from the building into the street and stared up at our windows and yelled at us with pure wrath. I leaned out and sang back, Hallelujah!

It is no great confession to say that the truth is my little troupe and I were terrible, beyond terrible; there were cats that pled with us to stop screeching. I spent what was left of my earnings, desperate to get us to a point that warranted any hope of auditioning well should we have the chance to perform for Ford and Kunkel. After many long months of screeching we were turned out by our landlord and our furniture and instruments were seized. I was completely ruined, devastated.

Two of my friends were staying at the rooms of an aunt and I was looking for someone to blame for sabotaging my dreams. I went to that woman's place already brewed for fighting and I stepped in her open door and found the quiet living room with its braided rug and the brown daguerrotypes of stiff family members lined up on the desk under the thick mirror and I saw my own face floating there, covered in dust. I heard something from the bedroom and I walked in without speaking. On the bed my two friends were naked, sleeping. They lay on top of the sheets. Their bodies were shining with sweat. The hand of one rested on the shoulder of the other. The intimacy hit me like a stroke in my brain. I felt hatred well up in me. That hatred was the expelled gas of my punctured dreams under so much pressure. I took the heavy lamp beside the bed and smashed it down on one of their faces. To this day I don't remember which one I hit or what I thought while doing it. He woke screaming and so did my other friend. They wrestled me to the floor. I was possessed and spitting every kind of foul word I could find. They threw me out and locked the door and I cried in the hallway leaning on that door, knowing I was wrong and no one loved me.

I am so ashamed even now that I can only remember for a second what his face looked like with his nose pushed over his cheek and his upper lip split open, and then it hurts too much and I push it away, but it always returns. My grandmother used to say to me that as you go through life you should try to injure as few people as possible. I thought she was talking Jesus but she meant it literally. She meant that it is hard to be good but it is important to be good. I failed her in that too.

That day I saw a poster for a show featuring a woman in men's clothes with a pistol in each hand. She was an Indian named Pauline with long black hair, bear claws in a necklace around her throat; she was the secret dream and the manifest terror of her audience. I stood for minutes and looked at the woman, who I felt a strong affinity for. I thought if I could be like her and have a stage of my own, I would change the world and row on row of white people would applaud until their hands bled. When the spell broke I sucked down my disappointment and my rage and I left town alone.

I worked the trains, singing and dancing in the aisles and selling newspapers and water until the middle of summer of 1876 when cholera became so prevalent in the Western cities that I thought it prudent to retire. In this way I managed to avoid the Ashtabula Horror, although I can still picture myself standing in the aisles hearing the great cracking of the bridge fracture and I can feel myself falling, falling with all those strangers into a watery abyss. I remember it because it was my fate in some other life.

After some indecisiveness, I settled in Jefferson City. One evening I strolled into the Diamond Mine, and, stepping to the bar, which came up to my juvenile shoulders—I was, by then, five foot tall—I demanded of the bartender if he had any good pale brandy. He waited a second and said that he had. The patrons all leaned in to hear me order. I told him in an imperative tone to give me a ten-cent drink, and none of his instant-death kind, either. This made a sensation among the colored swells seated at the fashionable tables at the back. They took my swaggering to be the real confidence of a tiny man and thought me dangerous, but I was just sick and tired, and pale brandy had been prescribed to me as the best preventative of cholera. I swallowed my drink, paid for the brandy, was preparing to go when I heard this dialogue behind me.

Who, for pity's sake, is that?

That? That there is just the boy you want!

Turning, I saw a couple of swells sitting together at the end of the room. One of them called me over and introduced me to Johnny Booker. Now, I had heard the songs then popular: "Meet Johnny Booker in the Bowling Green" and "Johnny Booker Help Dis' Nigger," and when I was aware that I was standing before the person to whose glory these songs were written, it was difficult to hold my jellied skeleton upright. I looked on this man as unquestionably the greatest Negro minstrel, the greatest man on earth. I felt about him the way Calamity Jane felt about Wild Bill; I would have borne his children.

In the course of a few minutes I was conducted to a backroom where I was made to dance juba to the time Johnny Booker kept by clapping his hands. He loved me! I was engaged on the spot and made a jig-dancer with a weekly salary of five dollars and all my expenses paid.

You can't imagine the excitement with which I prepared for the stage. Napoleon in his coronation robes was not prouder or happier than I was in my flannel knee-pants, corked face and woolly wig, bowing for my audience. That first show I was called out for three encores. I do not remember any embarrassment, only a superior joy at filling the house and dancing in front of more heads than I could count. The day after my first performance I saw a poster of myself with one arm and one leg elevated in the act of performing juba over a miniature city. I was dancing over the heads of passersby, over the carts and carriages, over the bridges and churches. I was an angel. I was godlike.

It was glorious. I met and was equal to many other performers, some of whom I had admired for a long time, some of whom were famous! I felt the equal of the president and I know I could have shook his hand with pride if he could be seen at a Negro show.

The first part of our performance we gave with whitefaces. I played a little Scotch girl in plaid petticoats, who executes the Highland fling. By practicing all day most days I came to understand my role and even to resent the world from the point of view of a little redhead. I learned to spin and knock and toss about the tambourine on the end of my forefinger. At last, as the Scotch girl, I was promoted to be one of the end men in the first part of the performances. In addition to my jig I now appeared in all sorts of *pas de deux.* I took the principal parts in Negro ballads, and danced "Lucy Long." I am told I was enchanting.

In the end, I think I understood Calamity Jane so well because we were like mirror images of each other, one dressed as a woman and the other as a man, one loving the stage and the other being trapped there. We were both wanderers with itchy feet and all manner of broken hearts and families behind us. We neither of us knew what regular life could offer. You might as well have put shackles on me as made me live in a house and you might as well have caged her as made her sleep away from the sky. At any rate, we wandered all over the Far West, traveling at all hours of night and day. The life was so exciting and I was so young; I was as happy as an itinerant mortal can be.

I met Dirty Em in a small town near Topeka. She joined the troupe for a few nights and played the comic roles, the ones that only required the look of a woman and not my training. Em was loud and beautiful and she could beat any of us at cards. She drank and in order to get close to her I tried to drink too. She scraped me up and took me home and in the morning I asked her to marry me. Shortly thereafter we began to drink and fight like it was a professional act. Which is to say we lacked the natural limits such as real people put into effect to keep from killing each other. She called me names and threw things and I shook her like a damn doll. We didn't even make love. We made hate. One day she threw a gun at me, screaming, why did I ruin her life? I came along and made a nothing out of her. Why did I destroy her dreams and humiliate her and why didn't I just kill her? I admit I was completely drunk and it was only ten o'clock in the morning. She scratched my face and punched me in the groin and grabbed a knife and then somehow I shot her. I was a terrible shot and I only grazed her wrist with the first bullet, but with the second one I tore her cheek open. She stood there with her hand over the wound looking as if she held her face from sheer amazement.

Please, I said, I'm sorry.

I spent the next year in jail. She came to see me and we were calm with each other, survivors of something together. But when I finished my sentence I left without telling her, getting on the train as I had so many times and leaving.

I felt bad about shooting my wife, but not as bad as I felt

about hitting my friend back in Toledo. But then he was asleep and she was awake; he was innocent and she was at least partly to blame for giving me the gun. I did not know how to find my troupe or if they were still together. I went farther West than I ever had before, trying to find something different in myself that matched the landscape. I half thought I could finish school and get married again and maybe have a few kids. Once in a while I could picture that life clearly, like my death on the train; it was a memory from another life.

I arrived in Deadwood still a young man. I walked down the streets and found the Bella Union. I walked in and got myself another job dancing and singing as a player in someone else's show. I liked Deadwood. There was a church for every saloon. The gold-bugs and the preachers walked hand-in-hand down to the river for baptisms. Chinese lanterns hung in half the shop windows and the colored folks lived right downtown.

I made friends with your mother, who, for all her drinking, had the ability to see inside people and forgive them. And I made friends with Sam Fields, the Nigger General, and he told me about his service in the 114th Infantry Division, how he was a private with the attitude of a general when asked to stand up for his people. He told me about being a farm laborer after the war and making the decision to give it up and come to the Hills to pan for gold. Sam was intelligent and he knew his history (they also called him the Darkey Shakespeare) and he liked to orate on the great black men of America: Nat Love, known as Deadwood Dick, a famous cowboy; and Bill Pickett, the great bulldogger out of Texas. Years later Sam and I would celebrate Edward McCabe being elected state auditor in Texas and then again in Kansas where he established the all-black town of Langston. And we cheered because Langston was named by McCabe after John Mercer Langston, the first African-American Congressman elected from Virginia. The world was changing and we were there to see it together.

Deadwood was an international oasis. Its Chinatown, in fact, was big and getting bigger. People said it was the biggest Chinatown beside San Francisco, and the whites could no longer pretend they were alone. Nights I was offstage I went with Calamity and Sam to eat some Chinese food and talk with the old fellow, who reminded me of my grandfather, that cheery man who pinched my grandmother's behind until one day he got himself shot by one of those clumsy men who shoot other men by accident. Cause of death: mischief unknown. On the odd occasion, when we were very lucky, we'd see a lion-dance in the place, two people performing acrobatics under the giant gold head trailing red ribbons. Calamity cheered and howled; she was so happy when the cymbals crashed.

Our other friend was Aunt Sally Sarah Campbell, a col-ored woman who came in as a cook for Custer and bought herself a mining claim. She was the first woman to do that and white men were proposing marriage to her when the gold came in. The journalists made up a new name for what Sally was; they called her an unbleached American. The four of us thought that was hilarious. Sally said it was like saying she was as good as a white. Calamity said it was like saying she was a man. I thought, how strange it was for white people to see their own skin as bathed in acid. Sally made us dinners some-times and we talked business, asking her advice. She was a stone-solid woman with a confidence I envied. Later, in

Galena, she cooked to feed the poor miners, always sharing her good luck. Calamity delivered the food because the men had seen so few black faces not made that way by coal that Sally feared they might not eat. She and Calamity were ever colluding in kindnesses.

So many of my old associates in the cork opera had already passed away. To a quieter stage, I hoped, beyond the double-dealing of managers and fickle audiences. An old showman is, in truth, a being *sui generis*, something unlike any other. We were like the heroes of the Far West, a dead and dying breed able to make the most dramatic of forms out of the most minor of incidents. We were not naturally worse than the majority of men when it came to lying, liquor and love, but we experienced more temptation and so we fell more often and became known more for our weaknesses than our strengths.

My second wife, Mollie, knew me to be a man of contradictions, and, as she was a kind and generous profiteer of human flesh, we understood each other and were most gentle with each other always.

I performed on Mollie's stage for three years. Towards the end of that time I was tired of the excesses of life. I began to doubt whether a great Negro minstrel was a more enviable man than a great senator or author. I wondered if I could be one of those things instead. Mollie loved me. She would have turned over every cent made by her girls upstairs to keep me dancing in the gaming hall. I had her purchase books for me and I began to study every day, devouring every work of poetry, biography, fiction and history I could lay hands on. I practiced arithmetic and grammar in the day and I dressed up like a good Scotch girl at night.

Week by week I became indifferent to the audience. Then I began to feel contempt fester until finally I felt a positive hatred of their vacant faces. They would feel the same, I thought, watching me dance, as they would staring at a puppet in a museum.

The community made the decision for me. They finally found out I had been in prison for shooting my first wife and I was marched out of town and left by the railroad tracks. Mollie, Sam, Calamity and Sally tried to stop them. But I was happy to be released from the security of the Bella Union.

My life, in the end, consisted of more treks and visions. A few times I went to school, a few times I held down jobs in stores or on ranches. But I always returned to show business. I traveled on steamboats, one that carried a museum with the Twelve Apostles, Jesus, Mary and Joseph all in wax and one that showcased a taxidermy zoo and was filled with stuffed birds, a giraffe and alligators. I performed beside the giraffe for a small wage. I belong on a stage no matter what size, and when you find a place where you feel you belong it is almost impossible to leave.

Martha

|||||||||||||||||||||||||||||||||||||||||||||

THE STAGE, THE FLOOR, THE WALLS, THE CHAIRS were all of the same newly hewn fragrant pine. Heavy red velvet curtains parted and a woman stood in the light emanating from a semicircle of gold painted shells. She wore fringed buckskin trousers and a cream-colored silk blouse. Her blonde hair, waved and clipped, shone as if oiled. She licked bright lips and put the back of one hand to her cheek. She opened her arms as Calamity Jane and sang to the body of her lover, Wild Bill, where he lay, stage left, a neat form outlined by a white sheet. Her voice was a sweet emotional treble.

> I have lov'd thee dearly lov'd thee,
> Through an age of worldly woe,
> How ungrateful I have prov'd thee,
> Let my mournful exile show,
> Ten long years of anxious sorrow
> Hour by hour I counted o'er
> Looking forward till tomorrow.
> Ev'ry day I lov'd thee more.
> Ev'ry day I lov'd thee more.

Pow'r nor splendor could not charm me.
I no joy in wealth could see.
Nor could threats or fears alarm me,
Save the fear of losing thee:
When the storms of fortune press'd thee
I have wept to see thee weep,
When relentless cares distress'd thee,
I have lull'd those cares to sleep.
I have lull'd those cares to sleep.

I have lov'd thee dearly lov'd thee

Miette

‖‖‖‖‖‖‖‖‖‖‖‖‖‖‖‖‖‖‖‖‖‖‖‖‖‖‖‖‖‖‖‖‖‖‖‖‖

Lew rode me to Billings and delivered me to a hotel. He walked me inside, holding my arm, smiling back at hostile and astonished stares. He rang the bell for the porter even though the man stood in front of us.

Dear sir, said Lew, could you call on my wife, Mollie Johnson? Tell her I am here with our child.

The porter sneezed loudly and blew his nose, hiding behind the handkerchief for as long as possible.

You make a fool of me, sir, he said at last.

A loud voice coming from the direction of the restaurant said, I liked whoring; I won't deny it. I met the best women in the world in the business!

That's Mollie now! Lew said, grabbing my arm and leaving the porter sneezing behind us and customers lining up to chorus, Well, I never!

Mollie! Lew called from the entrance to the restaurant.

A fat woman with blonde hair piled over her crown and around her ears and loading her shoulders looked up at us and her expression turned from dull confusion to joy.

Lew! Lew, come in! Don't mind the riff-raff. Come right in.

After whispers and embraces Lew left me with Mollie, who took me to her rooms. Alone, she was quiet and polite.

I'm sorry for what you heard, she said. Once in a while the hypocrisy of life makes me break out of this disguise. She gestured to the room and to her furniture and to herself. The room was clean and well decorated; a four-poster bed made up neatly with quilts stood at one end. The walls were papered in soft patterns. Pink velvet sitting chairs under an open window framed a little table that bore a silver tea set. A neat wooden bureau lined with framed pictures, brushes and combs, and a set of lace doilies stood against the far wall.

I live here now, Mollie said.

In the daylight that fell through her windows I saw that her face was old and it seemed the more so for the youthful style of her powdered makeup.

Do you like my dress? she asked, and I realized I had been staring.

Yes.

Yes? It was imported from Rome. This is real silk.

She stepped forward and took my hand and laid it on the voluminous skirt. The fabric was indeed soft as a chick's feathers and the violet color had a curious, shifting depth.

So, you don't know what to say to me now?

I don't. Except, I—I am looking for Calamity—

Jane, she said. Well, she is most likely in the Black Hills. She always returns there. She was always lovesick, stupid as a poet over the Badlands and Black Hills. Not me! I tell you the first time I got out of the coach with my mother I looked at the mountains and they reminded me of great crested waves. The Plains seemed endless like the ocean and I got seasick!

Mollie motioned for me to sit down and so I settled in a chair and watched her prepare tea. I felt numb; I don't know why. She poured for me and for herself and she settled in the opposite chair, took off her hair and the heavy beaded jewelry around her neck and ears, and sighed, looking out the window.

So, you are the girl, she said. Amazing. And she is your mother. You know, I came here, to the West, with my mother. We came all the way from Europe. My mother was as opposite yours as diamonds are opposite to coal. No offense, darlin.' I loved Jane. But my mother had such class ambitions! It was our intention to open a dress shop in America to serve all the suddenly wealthy with extravagances. We, like everyone, had heard that gold dust was common as dust motes. My mother got very sick on the journey from Germany to New York to Harrisburg to Lincoln to Deadwood. When she stepped down from the coach and said, Mollie, look we're here, I looked at her sunken eyes and I knew she would be dead in a day.

Dead from what? I asked.

Cholera. It was cholera. On the ship it had been so bad people liquefied before my eyes. In the morning I saw a woman delicately hold a handkerchief over her nose and that afternoon the same woman was tossed overboard by her husband. I don't understand why I could wade through that mealy rice-water diarrhea and not get sick but a doctor told me once it was something to do with my blood type. I have tough blood.

I had my mother's sewing machine, which she had held onto on the rocking boat through storms and plagues and undersea monster attacks. And I had a little room in the south end where I sat and worked most days and night. I made beautiful shirts and pants that could make a woman fall in love with the man that wore them. But I made dresses very poorly and everything else worse. I made a wedding dress once that killed the bride. She tripped on the hem coming down the stairs to go to the church and would probably have broken her neck falling except the veil wrapped round her throat and caught on a nail and hung her. So, business was up and down.

And then, one day, Calamity Jane came in and asked me to make a pair of trousers so fine they could bring a sheriff to leave his actress wife. I knew she meant to give them to Wild Bill. The pants I made were dark brown wool with a V-back waist and three bone buttons on the fly. I sewed one of Jane's own eyelashes into the crotch seam. I should have known then that she would be destroyed by the man in those beautiful pants. Anyway, I am at base a kind person and so I turned to whoring. I thought to save some lives that way. She laughed at her own joke and stood and smoothed her dress.

It is easy, she said in sudden seriousness, to judge a woman for half of what she's done without weighing it against the other half. Your mother begged money for drinks. She would borrow five dollars, buy a few drinks and then one for the house. She would go out on the street and borrow some more. She would order the house to buy and the house bought. This was tolerated, encouraged. It was considered neither begging nor borrowing. Calamity was Calamity; she was dear for being true; there was not an iota of herself that she kept hidden. I admire her for that. It was part of the expenses of the night to keep her glass filled and I must say that I was paid well for my pretty kindnesses and she was paid poorly for all the lives she saved, for all the good she gave, willingly to anyone. If you but whispered of a sick friend she would sober up and devote herself to their care. She risked her own health doing so. So, fine, she drank her weight the rest of the time. If Wild Bill Hickok was a hero then Calamity Jane was a hero and heroes were part of the overhead. I'll send a telegram to Dora DuFran, she said. Dora will know where to find your mother.

Dora DuFran

||||||||||||||||||||||||||||||||||||||||||||||||||

CHARLIE UTTER HAD THE MAD LOVE FOR DORA DuFran even though she was married and it made his friends, especially Martha, laugh to see him so besotted. Charlie, Martha always said, was the most noble of creatures in all forms of love including friendship, and little interested in public opinion. The only person who may have loved Wild Bill more than Martha Canary was Charlie Utter. He followed and protected Wild Bill as the tiger follows and protects a spoiled cub. Once Bill was gone the only person who could make him laugh was Dora.

Charlie was no joke of a lover. He cut a notable figure. He stood only five and a half feet tall but he was unusually meticulous in his person. He had long flowing gold hair and a trimmed moustache. He wore hand-tailored fringed buckskins, fine linen shirts, beaded moccasins and a large silver belt buckle, elaborated with designs of roses and thorns, and he carried a pair of gold, silver and pearl ornamented pistols. He slept under the highest quality blankets, imported from California, and he carried with him everywhere mirrors, combs, razors and whisk-brooms. He was well known for his bizarre habit of bathing daily and the whiff of lotions that followed him.

So, when Dora gathered Martha to a room and told her

friend (all flapping and flushed) that Charlie had asked her to marry him and that she had declined on the basis of her matrimonial state, Martha thought it natural to advise him to treat Dora's every request from then on as a heroic task set by a goddess to win her immortal favor. Charlie, understanding how little he understood, agreed to such a long-term courtship that it might never be clear what was won by whom or how or when.

It was fall in 1878 when Dora thought of the cat solution. Martha, she said, I have it! My girls are the sweetest, the prettiest and the cleanest in Deadwood. But because they are, they are also the loneliest, so much more discontented than the girls who work for Madam Mustachio, who are always gay with drink, or even the girls who work for Mollie Johnson, who are so prone to jealous fistfights. I know now they need a cure for their loneliness as much as or more than they need other cures.

Dora sent her pianist and lawyer, Franca, to ask at the *Black Hills Pioneer* office where they could get some pets for the girls. Franca was followed down the street by a band of suffragists beseeching Franca to abandon Dora's whores and the men who drank liquor beside them.

Now suffrage came to the West years before it came to the East. Wyoming gave women the vote in 1869. New Jersey and New England actually gave the vote to women earlier, but that was by accident. They forgot to recognize a difference between citizens in the laws. Many of the wives in town were suffragists and by and large they did not like either Dora or Calamity Jane. You can guess what they thought of soiled doves and ladies dressed as men. They clashed. But they were on the same side regarding political representation. Women lawyers were being admitted to the bar in California, Wyoming and Colorado, and Franca had come to Deadwood from Wyoming. Maybe it was because Deadwood was so lawless and events so rarely came to court—a citizen was more likely to see a doctor than a judge after a dispute—but no one ever bothered Franca. Or maybe it was because the town liked having a real lawyer who lived there, even a woman, even if she only played piano.

Dora told Franca the girls needed some uncompromising love. You see, said Dora, I have my parrot, Fred, who eats out my mouth and tells me all the time that I am wonderful. So I know what a difference even a little bit of animal love can make.

Franca went into the office of the *Pioneer* and said, My name is Franca Gordon and I'd like to place an advertisement. Richard Hughes, a reporter for the newspaper, was working that day and he asked what type of ad should be placed. Franca was very proper. She dressed like a church lady, all dark colors, high collars and straight sleeves. She was broomstick skinny with bulging eyes. She was so grave everyone listened to her, afraid to miss the news of their own death. In her most professional voice she said, I wish to purchase a dozen cats.

What are you going to do with a dozen cats? Mr. Hughes asked.

Rodents, said Franca. She explained that she was an attorney who presently was employed as a piano player at Dora DuFran's Green Front Hotel. And, like the other establishments on lower Main Street in Deadwood Gulch, the Green Front was crawling with rats. This was only partly true. Dora was particular about keeping the rooms immaculate but outside the kitchen, in the alley, where the garbage collected, there were, undeniably, inevitably, rats. Consequently, said

Franca, the ladies are unable to concentrate on their work and the customers are complaining.

Hughes claimed there were no cats or rats in Deadwood. He said they had some rats before but some magic evening they all wandered into the forest and coyotes got them. He was the sort who thought if he did not know a thing it was not true. Franca lifted her tight little hat and adjusted her hairpins. Now, she said, that is frustrating. I am sorry to say that I have seen the rats. They are most real and it is essential I locate and purchase at least a dozen cats. Do you know anyone who could bring some cats into town?

Mr. Hughes, in spite of his doubts, thought for a second, then told her Charlie Utter would be pulling out for Cheyenne to buy supplies soon and he might be able to accommodate. I'll take you to Charlie, he offered.

Had I known, said Franca, you would direct me to Charlie Utter, Dora would have gone herself.

Left alone with Charlie, who was a friend to all, Franca was honest and explained Dora's plan to put a cat in each of the Green Front rooms.

Well, I am moved, said Charlie, by her sensitivity, her human compassion. My God, she is an angel! Please tell Dora I will procure the finest felines and deliver them forthwith.

Well, in no time at all Charlie traveled and when he returned he delivered a wagonload of purring cats, and soon the Green Front was the only completely rat-free building, much less brothel, in Deadwood. The girls were happy, the customers were happy, Dora was happy, and after a small reciprocal gesture, Charlie was happy too.

But Madam Mustachio was not at all happy watching customers line up for the Green Front. She went to Al

Swearengen and Mollie Johnson and asked that all the brothel-owners in town join forces to put pressure on the mayor and city council to bring legal action to stop the public nuisance created by crowds forming at the Green Front. Evidently, the clerk didn't understand what was going on. He drafted an ordinance that outlawed houses of prostitution within the city limits. Well, this had Al and Mollie stomping and crying bloody murder. But by that time the wives of the town had discovered the mistake and they were overjoyed, insisting the ordinance be passed as written.

Dora was fit to kill and suddenly all the brothel-owners were again on the same side even if it was the wrong side of the town. But no matter what fuss they made, no matter the deadly threats implied by Al Swearengen or the secrets to be revealed by Mollie Johnson, city hall was packed with spectators when the law was unanimously adopted. Franca and the girls carried Dora, screaming, out of the hall. Franca tried to staunch her employer's fuming. Dora, she said, you have to trust me. Now I can prove that I'm not only a great pianist; I'm also a great lawyer. Dora slapped Franca and stormed home. Franca stayed in good spirits right behind her.

The next day the law went into effect and the sheriff arrived at Dora's door. She was allowed to stay at the Green Front under house arrest until her trial the following Tuesday. Dora was on her way to trial the next day when Charlie appeared. Charlie stood in front of her braced in his finest posture and cleared his throat. Dora, he said, could I ask you to please give Franca a message in response to her inquiry?

Sure, why not? Dora snapped. I've got nothing important to do. What do you want me to tell her?

Just let her know that I'll have my wagon parked where

she told me to, Charlie said and he bowed and walked away. Dora was too irritable and distracted to give what he said much thought. She walked into court, gave Franca the message in her best damn-you-all-to-Hell voice and stood before the judge.

That judge was as indignant as Dora was unrepentant. He waved the piece of paper that the ordinance was written on in the air and demanded the defense. Franca stood beside Dora, excited at last to be acting as a lawyer.

Miss DuFran, said the judge. *Yew*, he whined, are charged with violating the city ordinance that prohibits houses of prostitution. How *do* you plead?

Before Dora could start swearing, Franca answered. Your Honor, the accused pleads not guilty and waives her right to a jury trial.

Dora had thought a jury was a grand idea, given how popular the Green Front was. The judge turned to the city attorney and asked if he was ready to proceed. He was and so Dora watched as wife after wife testified to the noise and danger caused by the men waiting their turn outside the Green Front doors. No matter how many times Dora poked her, Franca declined to cross-examine any of them.

Eventually the smug prosecutor rested. Franca rose and ambled like a lioness up to the bench.

Your Honor, I move that the charges against my client be dismissed for lack of evidence, she said. Even Dora gasped.

There was a buzzing in the courtroom as if a beehive had erupted. Naturally, there were many madams and prostitutes in the crowd as interested parties. The judge pounded his gavel for a full minute to quiet the spectators. Miss Gordon, he said at last, do you take me for a fool? Kindly explain your argument.

Franca bowed to him slightly. Thank you, Your Honor. My reason is quite simple. A house of prostitution must be inhabited by prostitutes.

So? said the judge.

Franca pointed to the prosecutor. The prosecution has established the popularity of my client's place of business. However, he failed to prove that the popularity of the Green Front Hotel is due to its being a house of prostitution. I assure you that it is not such a house.

The judge fairly roared. If the Green Front is not a whore-house, then what the hell is it? he demanded.

Franca smiled. I sincerely appreciate your indulgence, Your Honor. And I understand the error. But the Green Front is a zoological exhibit, a residence for felines, very special, very precious felines. In fact, Miss DuFran is so fond of these furry sweet little four-footed friends that she provides a personal guardian for each and every one of them.

Everybody laughed. Dora sank in her chair and seethed with embarrassment. The judge banged on the desktop with his gavel. When the hullabaloo abated, he stared at Franca.

She stepped closer to the bench. In a loud, clear voice she said, Sir, if I'm not mistaken, it was just a few days ago I observed you during your visit to the Green Front. You were holding and petting Miss Trixie's little black pussy in the drawing room.

The judge fell back in his chair. His wife stood up in the gallery with her arms crossed over her chest. Franca turned to the courtroom as she said, I'm sure, Your Honor, we all know you would not have been in the Green Front Hotel if you did not also share Missus DuFran's love for cats. You see she provides an outlet for all the town's citizens by hosting such a vast array of loving creatures.

The judge lowered his head for a moment, then looking up with a queer smile he tapped his gavel and made his ruling.

After reviewing the facts, I find this ordinance is not applicable to cat houses, he said. Case dismissed!

Charlie Utter pushed through the crowd and announced in a loud voice, On the corner of Main and Wall streets, I have available for a limited time, one hundred and eighty-five of the finest felines ever seen in Deadwood Gulch, selling for a price of just fifty dollars each!

Martha

‖‖‖‖‖‖‖‖‖‖‖‖‖‖‖‖‖‖‖‖‖‖‖‖‖‖‖‖‖‖‖‖

S̲HE TRAVELED TO COEUR D'ALENE IN IDAHO AT least twice. She followed the stream of gold miners and lost soldiers, the two hundred men a day who arrived in the mining region in the spring of 1882. She left the railroad with the other women at Rathdrum and took a stagecoach along the Coeur d'Alene River and then from Kingston rode horse-back to Jackass.

Hell, she exclaimed. I could have gone to New York and back in the time it took to get to Jackass!

From Jackass Junction she crossed the divide into Beaver and Eagle City. It was in Eagle City that she performed for the first time.

The night began in a long tented barroom. Bloody angels in the snow made clear the sort of crowd she could expect. Whisky was fifteen cents a shot and the shots were passed hand to hand over the heads of the already drunk crowd. The bartender's head glittered with gold dust from his casual hands pinching the correct amount from miners' pouches and then running his fingers through his hair. Later, he would pan his bathwater. There was an orchestra of four fiddlers dressed in matching plaid suits and black hats and a semicircle of a stage separated from the crowd by calico curtains. The fiddlers played "Life Let Us Cherish," "Till Death Sounds the Retreat," "All's Well," "The Sisters" and other popular songs. The smallest fiddler was struck in the forehead by a flying glass and put down his instrument to appeal to the audience.

LADIES! GENTLEMEN! he cried. We are not tin monkeys before you. We are real entertainers. Show us some respect.

One musician put aside his fiddle and blew a trumpet to announce a change in program. The curtains parted and on the stage stood Martha in woollen pants and a jacket. She had a gun at one hip and a lasso on the other.

Everybody dance! she commanded. The fiddlers began a waltz and the women and men parted into two factions on either side of the room. The pretty girls were soon drawn to the floor by the Beau Brummells. There were far more men than women and so a system of turns was silently established and the women were handed neatly off at musical intervals. Of course this system was abused and short tempers erupted and fights broke out, though the dancing continued. Blood spatters across the walls were wiped away assiduously by the bouncers. Light from the hanging lamps swung softly over the moving figures.

Jane watched. When the inertia finally set in and the remaining celebrants were quiet, draped over chairs or slumped by the walls, she began a monologue about her life. They listened, through bleeding ears, and watched, through swollen eyelids. She was young and her profile clear-cut, her whole countenance resolute and defiant. She wore lifts that made her tall as an elk. Her hands, spinning the lasso by her feet, or juggling knives to make her point, were so quick they were almost invisible. Impersonating a grizzly bear she growled so effectively the little fiddler and several women in the crowd screamed. She seemed to the unschooled miners, the bullwhackers, the gamblers, and even to the prostitutes, to be a thing beyond Creation—both awesome and bizarre.

She began her speech.

You may have heard of Old Two-Toes, the grizzly that has haunted the Dakotas for a dozen years. I had heard of her and seen the one survivor of her attacks: a man missing one eye, one cheek, half of his lower jaw and an arm. This man had to hold his face closed while he drank or chewed. His jaw made a terrible grinding sound whenever he moved it. He told me by Indian signs one night over cards about the attack and how he had seen the paw of the beast descend upon his face, the two claws more than enough to gouge out his eye and leave the wet jelly of it running down his neck.

I pitied this man and bought him his dinner and a night upstairs with a blind girl. But I have never been afraid of beasts, human or otherwise, so when I was asked by a friend to join him fishing in the area I thought of the bear, but only briefly.

My friend Su is a Chinaman. He runs a laundry but he is also an artist who paints images of the Black Hills the way they rise out of smoky mist; his pictures are so lovely they might be the patterns followed by the Creator. He asked me one day to join him on a trip and show him Spearfish Canyon. We were camping out by the water at night, fishing in the morning, and hiking all day. I was good at fishing and Su was a good cook. He treated me as a guide and paid me with liquor and cash. On the third day we spent the better part of the morning practicing with longbows.

After hours of target practice, shooting at trees, we set out on a hike. Snow had fallen overnight, and the hunting conditions were perfect because our steps were muffled. We climbed up, winding our way through the snow clouds. By mid-morning Su had downed a pretty doe. At my friend's insistence we said a brief prayer of thanks for the animal, then dressed it and hung it in a tree, planning to return the next day with help to carry it home.

The sun rose and warmed the hills, the early snow melted, and the woods were fragrant and very damp, making it easy to move along quietly over the soggy ground. We came to the top of the hill and I saw movement in the trees off to my left. At first it was a shadow, too hard to fathom. And then I saw Old Two-Toes facing me. At the sight of me she roared and I felt the air shake. She charged. She closed in on us with great strides. I remember seeing those gleaming eyes, and her high shoulders pumping as she ran. Su was twenty yards up trail, so I ran towards him, screaming, It's a bear, get away! But he was frozen, entranced. I couldn't leave him so I turned and for a minute the bear stopped. We swayed in each other's gaze. What a beautiful, magnificent, adult animal she was. So clean and healthy, maybe four hundred pounds. Clear eyes set in a broad forehead. Big black claws clutching the dirt. She was perfectly made to live in the hills. I thrust my bow at her and yelled at her, For Christ's sake, get out of here!

She lunged at Su, ignoring me and biting him in the face and neck. I could see, and so I could feel, his face ripping. Then I was on the sow's back. I heard her teeth crunching down on Su's head. I took my arrow and I climbed to her head. I heard Su screaming, She's killing me! She's killing me! And then I drove my arrow into her ear, and pounded the end to drive it deep into her brain. She fell on Su and he moaned but he was alive. I rolled the dead bear off of him and carried him all the way down the mountain and draped him over my horse and rode them back to town.

In Deadwood the lady doctor, Dr. Stanford, sewed Su's face back on. I trusted her the most because she had treated me for pneumonia, and because she trusted me with her daughter, sick little Emma, when she had to travel to care for folks. Su's own doctor, an elderly Chinese man who spoke no English, administered acupuncture to help manage the pain and herbs to stave off infection. The two doctors showed appreciation for each other. When Su awoke he assumed he was dead and he apologized to me for devising the trip. It's all right, I said. We're alive. He didn't understand and so I brought him a mirror. He looked at himself a long time and turned his face to see every angle.

I had to kill her, I said. I felt terrible about everything. He nodded and said a short prayer. He thanked me profusely and sent his attendant to bring me gifts, a painting of an enormous waterfall, a silk jacket and an orange. I had never tasted anything so bright, so much like childish joy.

THE AUDIENCE was silent when she finished. The room had emptied while she spoke. A few sleepers were draped over card tables or collapsed against the walls.

Calamity Jane spun her lasso at her feet and considered what to do.

Come and see me at the Pan-American Exposition, she said at last. Tired, she exited the stage by the side steps, walking through the bar to the door.

The Pan-American Exposition

The Exhibit of Human Nature

T HERE ARE WOMEN IN RUSTLING ROBES WHO DRIVE TO the Lincoln Park Gateway and view the fair through lorgnettes; and women in short skirts and shirtwaists who come in the trolleys and get much more for their money. There are thoughtful students and giggling girls. . . . There are brides and grooms who are bored by the crowds, and crowds who are delighted with the brides and grooms. There are strait-laced dames who could not show you the way to the Midway; and tight-laced dames who could not show you the way out of it; and fair American girls who would not know when they were in it; and types from Hawaii and the Orient that make a violent background for American womanhood. There is every type at the Pan-American Exposition that ever was known, and the harmonious blending of them all proves advancement in the material exhibits.

The first type that greets you is the gateman belonging distinctly to the Sphinx species. The second is one of an ambitious squad of boys, who informs you that a daily permit at fifty cents per diem is necessary for your camera. You declare it's an outrage; but you've got the Kodak craze, and deserve to pay. Mentally, you resolve to take all your pictures in one day. Actually, you bring the camera every day of your stay, making daily unsuccessful efforts to evade the squad. This type is the detective in embryo, and closely resembles a small animal known as the ferret.

Having paid for the privilege, the only way to get even with the management is to snapshot everything in the grounds. The first subject that appeals is a little old woman whose face is framed in a sunbonnet, which is framed in beds of tulips and orchids from a Long Island exhibitor's hot-houses. The little old gardener tells you her name is Mary, and she lives between the Exposition grounds and the poor-house, and has one hundred and two plants of her own, which she'll be glad to give you slips of; but things have been running down lately, and the pension's stopped since Johnny died, and Lucy's getting tall and expects to go out in company soon, so she wouldn't like to go to the city to work; and when it comes to working in the Exposition or working towards the poorhouse, why, the fairgrounds were like play—specially as she always did love flowers so.

Mary is a common type—but Mary's daughter is commoner.

After Mary and her flowers, one observes the Pan-American small boy—the same that we have always with us, except that he is without restriction, and the air of Buffalo agrees with him. He has a way of cutting across the flower-beds to shorten distances; and the state police, who overtake him without demolishing the flowerbeds, have a way of propounding the value of tulips and underrating the comforts of the town jail, which the small boy never forgets. These state police are a new type to the New Yorker, who is used to beef and brawn on the force. They are long, lean, muscular fellows with military bearing and uniform and intelligent faces.

There are also on the grounds camps of state troops and a small army of attachés for the exhibits in the Army and Navy Building. So the Exposition brass-button girl is happy and the type she adores gets the adulation on which it thrives. No building at the fair is so popular with the younger women as the Army and Navy Building; and no girl is so envied as she who happens to know an officer, who does the honors in one of those cozy little white tents, with chests containing everything you don't expect.

The building next in popularity to the Army and Navy is the Manufactures and Liberal Arts. Here women predominate, and it is curious to watch the different types of women linger around those features, which would naturally appeal to them. . . . There are old women and middle-aged women, neat women and shiftless women, thin women and fat women, and they all had housework wrinkles—little creases that settle about the eyes and mouth from little frets and worries. They crushed forward, trampling one another's toes and poking one another's ribs, and their eagerness was of the sort that characterizes a hungry dog's regard for raw meat. I knew it was a household implement before I heard a suave voice say: Ladies, it is so simple a child can use it. Other washers tear the clothes; ours will wash lace curtains without pulling a thread, or cleanse a carpet with ease. You can do a six weeks' wash of an afternoon with our machine, and find it as pleasant as a matinee. Come, madam, let me send you one on trial. You look as if you would appreciate it. The woman addressed was small and wiry, and the housework wrinkles looked as if they were there to stay. Her admiring gaze was lifted from the washing machine to the man's face, as she said earnestly, It looks like it would be such a comfort.

Comfort, madam? Why, our washing machine is unquestionably the first principle of a happy home. Let me send you one on trial free.

I guess I'll wait, said the little woman timidly.

Never get another chance like this, ma'am.

I'll speak to John about it.

Does John do the washing?

No, she says drearily. He doesn't; doesn't have to pay anything for tubs, either.

Whereupon all the women thereabout, who had been following the colloquy with the keenest interest, looked knowing and appreciative of this vindication of their downtrodden sex, and the crowd dispersed in high good humor.

In the center of the Manufactures Building was a gathering that defied classification. All types of women were huddled together, rich and poor, esthetic and commonplace. It was lunch-time, and they were engaged in the work of managing a free lunch. Women whose diamonds were gems and whose gowns were creations elbowed women who might have been their cooks, to get free biscuits made from the *finest baking-powder on earth*; free pancakes made from the only pancake flour that wouldn't result in sinkers; free soup from the only cans containing real tomatoes; free samples of all the varieties of mustard, jam and pickles; free sandwiches of minced meat; free cheese, preserves, chow-chow, plum-pudding, clam broth, baked beans and pickled lobster.

ANOTHER VARIATION of the schoolmarm type held forth in the Horticulture Building. She occupied a booth decorated with spheres, charts, maps and tracts, and tried to convince

Pan-American visitors that the earth's habitable surface is concave instead of convex. The crowd, whose tongues take on a kind of Exposition looseness, chafed her considerably and asked vital questions at the wrong moment, each time necessitating a fresh start. When the young woman at last was permitted to reach the end of her argument—which, fortunately, no one understood—an old lady asked pertinently what difference concavity or convexity would make to the folks living on the Earth, anyway.

It will make this difference, replied the young woman: we can prove that the earth is concave, while Copernicus never proved, but only supposed, the earth to be convex. Now if you start with a supposition, you have no solid foundation for your science, astronomy, religion or the relations of God and man. But if you start with knowledge—

What's knowledge got to do with religion? interrupted the old lady. Didn't the Lord say all you needed was faith?

Oh, faith is all very well, replied the expounder of Koreshanity, but knowledge is better.

Humph! said the old lady. You ain't married, be you?

ALL OVER the fairgrounds there seemed to be a dozen women to every man. From the Horticulture Building to the Graphic Arts to the Temple of Music, the Ethnology Building, the United States Government Buildings and across the beautiful Esplanade with its flowers and fountains, there were women, women, everywhere—old women in sedan-chairs propelled at fifty cents an hour; tired women in rickshaws pulled by Japs at a dollar an hour; athletic women in calfskin boots at only the cost of leather per hour.

The men, where were they? Packed like sardines in the

United States Fisheries Building, grouped in twos and threes and hunches, their backs to the exhibits, telling fish stories.

Don't think much of that line of trout, said a man with chin-whiskers. Why, up near our camp in the Adirondacks, we don't think anything of hauling them in weighing twenty to thirty pounds.

The man with the side-whiskers nodded absently and reckoned the trout on exhibition were as big as most trout grow.

The bass are rather cheap-looking, though, he admitted. We've got an island up in the St. Lawrence, and the bass up there certainly are wonderful! Great big fellows, and so plentiful they rise up in schools and bound over on the island, waiting to be cooked for breakfast.

Yes, assented a clean-shaven boy, who was his son, I've seen 'em come right alongside a brushwood fire outdoors and lie there till they were broiled.

The man with the chin-whiskers looked meditative.

Well, he drawled at length, I'm not much on bass. Angling for trout's the real sport, and the stream near us is just packed with 'em—great speckled beauties; and I never did see fish multiply so. Two years ago I caught a fairly good specimen. Managed to get it in the boat, but the head and tail hung out both ends. It was the end of July then, and we leave up there in September. I knew we couldn't finish eating that fish before we went back home, so what was the use killing it? I resolved to put it back in the stream; but before doing so, I tied a big blue ribbon in its tail. Now, do you know, that fish has grown to the size of a human in two years, and multiplied the trout in that stream by two or three thousand.

He of the side-whiskers stared and his son gasped

quickly. But you can't prove all those fish are the result of that same trout?

That's just what I can, said the man with the chin-whiskers, profoundly. Every one of those trout has a blue ribbon tied to his tail.

THREE-QUARTERS OF the people at the Fair had followed the same route. From the Beautiful Orient to the Indian Congress the streets were black with people—whites, blacks, Indians, Mexicans, Hawaiians, Japanese, Americans; all packed so closely together they merged into one composite type, whose chief characteristic was curiosity, whose motive-power was deviltry.

The atmosphere of the Midway is not conventional and a few inhalations produce immediate results, which are, first, a realization that Buffalo is a long way from home; second, a hallucination that nobody one knows will be met in this place, which seems so far removed from America; and third, a conviction that much knowledge may be gained from these representations of foreign countries and not one detail of the outfit should be overlooked.

Lavinia Hart
The Cosmopolitan
September 1901

Miette

〰〰〰〰〰〰〰〰〰〰〰〰〰〰〰〰〰〰〰

THE WOLF HOWLED, A LONG TUNNEL OF SOUND THAT fell off sharply without answer. I could see her through the trees, faced away from me, a dark figure standing, looking into something I could not see. Her thick tail twitched and she raised her face and cried.

I stirred my food on the fire. The light was flat and gray but it was far from dark. I took the postcards Lew had given me out of my pack and considered them. I looked at her face, her eyes, looking directly back at the camera but unseeing, not seeing me. I put away the other pictures and stared at the picture of her on her horse at the Pan-American Exposition. This picture was blurry but it was her, caught, in life. I knew this because of her posture, the way her hand held the reins, the power in her leg, her foot in the stirrup; she was stilling her dark horse. She was thin, the outlines of her body lost beneath a thick Western costume.

I remembered my father reading aloud to me from the newspaper we had picked up in town. It might have been the same day that photograph of my mother was taken.

U.S. President William McKinley has been assassinated.

I remembered mishearing him, believing that he had said the president was shot by a buffalo in the Temple of Music.

Martha

||||||||||||||||||||||||||||||||||||||||||||

PRESIDENT McKINLEY SPOKE TO THE CROWDS.
Expositions, he said, are the timekeepers of progress.
They record the world's advancements. They stimulate the
energy, enterprise and intellect of the people, and quicken
human genius!

Applause and stomping and cheers filled the air. The
magical system invented by Nikola Tesla lit the evening with
strings of glass bulbs that glowed brilliantly, hung everywhere between tall poles.

McKinley stepped into the audience, reaching for hands,
squeezing palms and fingers. He looked into the shining eyes
of his constituents.

It's a great day, he said. It's a great day for all of us.

His broad shoulders were patted and squeezed as he
levered his way through the crowd. His glasses fogged slightly
with sweat. A woman reached to stroke his face; he took her
hand and kissed it.

A slim man in a neat dark coat stepped into McKinley's
path. McKinley looked into the still pale eyes and then down
at a hand wrapped in a handkerchief pressing a gun into his
belly.

MARTHA STOOD outside the operating tent, pinched by the shifting shoulders around her. One onlooker shouted, The president's blood! pointing to a line of drops in the sand. Reporters swung towards the blood, exploding flashes in unison.

The interior of the tent was dark. The electrical lighting draped everywhere around the fairgrounds had not been installed in the emergency hospital. Edison was there with his X-ray machine, a black box like a coffin on wheels.

Use it to look for the bullet in his abdomen.

But instead the doctors looked at Edison's wrinkled face, his broken eye, the sores across his dying hand, and said, No, it is too dangerous.

Tears ran down McKinley's face. I remember you, he whispered to Edison. I saw you in the crowd. Good man.

Yes, I was there. You are going to be all right, Mr. President.

One doctor held a metal pan up to catch the sunlight and focus it on the little well above the president's navel. He moved to keep the light directed while another doctor dug through the blood and flesh, searching for the bullet. McKinley gasped and cried out.

The surgery continued, a stranger's fingers then hands still searching in the body of the president.

He looked into the surgeon's eyes and sputtered, Where's Ida? Where's my wife? Is Ida all right? Where are the damn lights?

Miette

〰〰〰〰〰〰〰〰〰〰〰〰〰〰〰〰〰〰〰〰〰

T HE ENGINE STEAM WAS BLUE, SPIRIT-LIKE, ROLL-
ing behind the train against the watercolor sunset.
Fountains of sparks flew from every wheel as the train ground
uphill. When the whistle blew I could taste the sound entering my teeth. I saw the brass headlamp cast light ahead of the
toothy V of the cowcatcher, and the brakeman standing on
the cab step holding out his red lantern, his shoes being
showered with white and yellow sparks. The carriages complained by squealing when the locomotive began to turn
along the rails that led to the next quiet station.

DORA DUFRAN had answered Mollie's telegram with an
urgent message to send me directly to Deadwood. I stalled for
a day and Dora sent another telegram, so I bought a ticket to
ride freight on the next train. The little card in my hand
seemed too small, too thin for what it offered me. I stood by
the rails and watched the train roll in, chuffing with an almost
human-sounding protest as it decelerated. It stopped, tall as
a building, in front of me, and the engineer leapt down and
went to have a cigarette. I walked up to a man taking tickets
and he looked at my ticket and looked at me.

Do you want to ride freight? he asked.

I don't know exactly what it means, I said.

It means you ride with the chickens.

I don't mind chickens, I said. I was afraid that he was suggesting I could not go on this train.

He laughed at me and clipped a little hole on my ticket. He called over to the ticketmaster in his booth, Tom, how full are we?

Not full at all, said Tom.

I can move you to coach and you can ride with the ladies in their car, if you like, he said kindly.

Thank you, I said feeling confused.

When I entered the ladies' car there was a murmur of shock and then a few soft laughs. I suppose that at first glance I looked and even smelled like a boy. The rough dirt under my fingernails and the stiff hairs all over my clothes were suddenly visible to me. I took a seat by a window at the front of the car near the door and tried to make myself smaller, less conspicuous. The windows were draped in striped navy curtains. The seats were padded and covered with worn black velvet. On the table in front of me was a little brass lamp with a tasseled gold shade. I could smell powder and perfume and other smells that were so unfamiliar I felt shame. I would have been better off with the chickens. My hand on the table was brown and dry. My nails were uneven and filthy. My boots had left a trail of muddy prints to my seat. I could not look the women in the face so I looked at their laps. Every one of them was clothed in shiny, layered skirts that ballooned around the hips. The skirts rustled persistently. The ladies held their hands neatly folded in their laps or else they held gloves, small books, bone fans, beaded purses, compact mirrors, even fuzzy gray kittens who batted at the lace peeking out from the long sleeves of the dresses. I rested my head on the windowglass and watched the landscape spinning by.

I saw the brass buttons of coyote pupils flicker by the tracks. They played sentinel, spaced at regular intervals along, watching the train pass by with interest. The stops were frequent and at each a woman got on and one got off. At about the fifth such stop a large woman got on. She was fussing loudly about the ticket-taker's blue eyes and his lovely smile. She swept past me and I saw her bustle, which seemed long enough to hide a horse. She turned in the aisle and faced me. She waved a fan by her neck. The effort of climbing the steps had made her sweat. She walked slowly back to me and bent down and took my chin in her gloved hand.

It is you, she said. I have a present for you from your mother.

The woman unpinned her hat and set it on the table in front of me. A great plume of pink feathers surrounded the brim.

I moved hell and high water to intercept you, she said. Do you know who I am?

No, I said.

I'm Dora DuFran. I made contact with friends on the rail to be sure I found you. I was afraid you would lose your nerve and disappear. I had to come and keep you going. I run the Green Front Hotel in Deadwood. Your mother is my very good friend. Can I sit here?

Yes, I said.

She settled across from me primping and plumping her outfit. She was stout with a bust so big and high she reminded me of a turkey. She had a pretty face framed in brown curls and her eyes were bright blue and heavily lined with charcoal that made the color stand out. Her lashes were curled and her cheeks were pinched pink; her lips were a darker pink. A lace collar hid a softened neck. Diamond bob earrings were clipped to her earlobes. She cocked her head to look at me.

What's the matter?

My God, you look like her and Bill both, and it is only now, looking at you, that I realize even I did not believe her.

Say her name, I said.

Martha Canary.

She has another name.

I know it. Calamity Jane.

Yes.

Yes. You are Calamity Jane's child. It's clear even from your rudeness.

I'm sorry.

Dora sighed and slid a card across the table. I turned it over. It was a calling card for her business. Printed on linen was the address, her name and a brief statement that read: *Come to the famous Cathouse, the Green Front Hotel, for comfort or companionship. We welcome you.*

As I said before, your mother is my truest friend. I promised her that I would give you something if I ever had the chance.

She opened a traveling bag and handed me a large envelope. It was creased and the paper had yellowed. The edges were furry with wear. I looked at her and opened the envelope with my thumbnail. I looked inside and saw that it contained a letter. I could go no further while she watched.

You need to see it.

I sat silently staring into the envelope while she fidgeted. At last she sighed and said, You've come a long way. I've come a long way too. I was born in Liverpool, England. Do I sound strange to you?

I nodded.

My accent is softer now. It's mixed in with the sounds I learned here. My husband says that I have an American snore. Come on now, this isn't a sad day.

I looked up, out the window, squinting at the white circle of the sun until my retinas ached.

That's a letter from your mother. Your mother has been my best friend for many years. I would venture that you must have some ill feelings towards her but I know the woman and I know what having you did to her. That's a letter she wrote just for you. I helped her with part of the writing. Belle Starr helped her with the rest, until Belle was shot. Do you know the Bandit Queen?

I shook my head and then my head shook the whole rest of me. The other women had gone quiet; they were listening. Dora fidgeted, pursing her lips as if she were deciding my fate.

Well, Belle was a good woman. Her family left Missouri after a Union attack. Her father's livery was burnt with all the animals in it. She got in with Jesse James and the Youngers. But she was a good woman. Your mother is a good woman too.

I don't know where I'm going, I said. I suddenly wanted off of the train. The women in the car were suffocating me with their sweet smells and rustling.

Well, you can always come by my place.

Are you inviting me to be a prostitute?

No, no. She shook her head and waved a hand at me. It's okay to be scared, she said. I would be scared. I'm sure your mother, as much as she wants it, is scared of the day she sees you. Listen to me, at her worst she is not the worst but at her best—she is amazing. I know you are angry and that's fair. But you had better see her now. She's not well. There will not be another chance.

I TRAVELED to Deadwood with Dora but I refused to speak to her again. All the resentment I had left in me was aimed at her for chaperoning the last leg of my journey and preventing my exit. I chose a small white hotel and took a room. I did not go to the Green Front. I needed some privacy to read what my mother had left me and to decide on my fate.

I left the windows open to draw some air in. I lit the black iron stove in spite of the heat and sat on a braided rug on the floor because the light from the little fire was better there. I let the sweat run into my eyes. I did not want to turn on a lamp in case anyone from the street should see me. My breathing was labored. My hands could barely operate. I turned over the pages and read her words. It seemed so strange that I could not hear, that I did not know, her voice.

Martha

||||||||||||||||||||||||||||||||||||||||||||||

The True Life and Adventures of Martha Burke
by
Martha Burke, aka Calamity Jane,
aka Your Mother

YOU WILL ALREADY KNOW THIS BUT YOUR FATHER was Wild Bill Hickok and my name was Martha Canary. I asked that you be named Martha and not Jane because Jane was never my name. Some people will tell you it was my middle name or that it was a name for a kind of woman like John is a name for a kind of man. But I want to tell you that you were named Martha after me.

I cannot tell you everything so I am choosing what I'd like you to know. For instance you should know that I am not writing this but speaking it. I cannot write or read. It is a great shame for me to tell you this. I asked that you be taught to read and write because I know how stupid, how crazy, looking at the letters and not knowing what they say makes me feel. It makes me feel the more stupid now when I am telling my life and not knowing really how it comes out. My friend, another woman like me, who shoots a lot, is writing this down. I will ask her to copy it and I will give it to people I trust and if you ever find any of them they will give you their copy. Believe me, whoever gives you this is my good friend, whatever history makes of us.

I was born in Princeton, Missouri. It was something we celebrated every May 1st, so I assume that is my birthday. If I have kept count right then I was born in 1852. My father and mother were natives of Ohio. I had two brothers, Elijah and Silas, and three sisters, Mary, Lena and Anne. I was the oldest. My mother died of washtub pneumonia in 1866 when I was fourteen. My father died of Salt Lake City when I was fifteen. I became then the mother of my five younger siblings.

As a child I always had a fondness for adventure and outdoor exercise and an especial fondness for horses. I began to ride at an early age and continued to do so until I became an expert rider. At ten I was able to ride the most vicious and stubborn of horses. In fact, the greater portion of my days and of my life in early times was spent on the backs of biters and buckers, and I loved it.

That was in Missouri. You see it was not all slave-keeping and war. The poor, and we were very poor, still had the big sky and the animals that ran over the earth and what we knew about roots and berries and how to fish. It was not like in the cities. We could live. But Missouri was burnt out after the war. There was so little left and so many memories of dead bodies, shot, burnt and frozen. I saw them in my dreams, lined up by picket fences. As soon as the war ended and people were free to move they moved West. The East was still divided North and South, steeped in what no one could believe had happened, not the politics anymore but the fresh recall of violence. Everyone was destitute. In the West the freed slaves, the disenchanted Union men, the guerrillas and countless impoverished Southerners came to a rough reckoning.

In 1865 we emigrated from our home by the overland route to Virginia City, Montana. It took five months to make the journey. My mother was still alive, although to think of it, she was weak and she coughed. On the way the greater portion of my time was spent hunting along with the men. In fact I was hunting whenever I was awake. In this way I became as good a shot as I was a rider. I could braid a rabbit's ears with bullets. At all times, with the men, there was excitement and adventures to be had. The women were hot and miserable, trying to keep their children clean and safe and laundry done and food cooked.

By the time we reached Virginia City I was considered remarkable. I was as good a shot and as fearless a rider as any boy my age. In fact my recollection of being a child was not that I was like a boy or a girl; instead I was like an animal that people praised for being useful.

I remember many occurrences on the journey from Missouri to Montana. Crossing the mountains the trails were in such poor condition that we often had to lower the wagons over ledges by hand with ropes. I was right there beside the men, burning my palms as we held on. The ground was so rough and rugged that horses were of no use.

Many of the streams in our way were noted for quicksand. The men told stories around campfires about how it looked like regular sand but if you stepped in quicksand it would suck you down and every move you made would pull you faster until you suffocated. Your best bet was to hold still until someone threw you a rope and pulled you out.

That, I said, cannot be true.

My father smacked me hard for talking back.

But there were places that were so boggy that unless we were very careful we would have lost horses and all. There were also the dangers brought by streams swelling on account of heavy rains. The men had a silent hierarchy that somehow told them who was the best to select where to cross the streams. There seemed to be no rhyme or reason to how they chose the spot. On more than one occasion I mounted my pony and swam across the stream several times merely to amuse myself while they plunged into the deepest parts after making a wrong decision. I did have many narrow escapes with my pony. Both of us almost washed away. But, as pioneers, we all had plenty of courage. In the end the group of us, dumb and smart, skilled and clumsy, overcame all natural obstacles and reached Virginia City.

Mother died at Blackfoot, Montana. Elijah and Silas cried, but me, Lena, Mary and Anne had too much to do. Lena made Mother a dress to be buried in. Actually, she finished a dress that Mother had been working on for weeks to wear at Christmas. We all had matching dresses that she had made first and we wore those to the funeral. Anne polished our brothers' shoes, Mary helped me make a meal. The little mite was a better cook at six than I will ever be. By seven she had as many little cuts and burns on her hands and forearms as our mother.

We left Montana for Utah in spring of 1866, arriving at Salt Lake City during the summer. Our father had drunk the equivalent of all the whisky he had abstained from during his marriage in the space of several months. When Mother was alive he was prickly but hard-working. After her death he was as removed from us as if he had gone with her. He might have come out of it but instead he died. We remained in Utah for a little while and then went to Fort Bridger, Wyoming Territory, where we arrived May 1, 1868. Then we headed on the UP

Railway to Piedmont, Wyoming. The answer to why we went anywhere was simple: money. There were six of us and only two (myself and Elijah) who were old enough to get paid for working even the most menial jobs.

We rode the railway, Elijah and me taking tickets and the others just filling in seats unless they polished shoes or carried bags for a few coins. We didn't sleep lying down until 1870.

Elijah and I joined General Custer as scouts at Fort Russell, Wyoming, in 1870. Up to this time I had always worn skirts and dresses, but Elijah had the bright idea that we could both join the army if we lied a little about his age and a little about my sex. The boys pitched in to show me some moves, walking and sitting, and farting and spitting. Sniff your own farts, advised Silas. Boys like to smell their farts. The whole thing entertained them greatly. Lena altered some pantaloons and a shirt and jacket for me. Mary cut my hair and Annie just sat there squealing with delight at my transformation. I was a good-looking boy, prettier like that than I was as the girl underneath. I interviewed well. I was young enough no one wondered about my voice.

Wearing a soldier's uniform was a bit awkward at first. It was stiff and heavy on my shoulders and legs, heavier than my skirts and blouses. Elijah and I commiserated about becoming men. But I soon got to be perfectly at home in men's clothes.

I had big plans for us and I spent many hours staring out at the coulees or counting eagles, imagining Elijah and me working side by side forever and Lena marrying a rancher and Silas working on the ranch with Lena's husband, growing up brown and muscular, and Mary becoming a schoolteacher and Annie a mother.

But Annie died in my arms of yellow fever and so did Mary and Silas. Elijah disappeared into the army and then into the prisons. Lena did marry a rancher, and that was the end of my family.

I went to visit Lena once, when I was pregnant with you. She laughed so hard she cried to see me waddle to the door with my potbelly hanging over my belt and my legs so bow-legged they might be a wishbone. And then she just cried when I asked her if she would take you. She cried at her kitchen table with her eight children like brown flowers turned towards the sun, looking on at their weeping mother. She said, Good Lord forgive me, I can't. I can't even feed all of these. I know it's my flesh and I love you, I do, so much, but I can't, Martha. I just can't. Good Lord, please forgive me.

It was then I looked at her and realized that she looked as broke as our mother in the days before her death, and I lied to her. I said I would keep you. We hugged and kissed each other a dozen times when I left. I turned back so many times my horse was confused. You were born in Sundance. A lady doctor who was my friend from Deadwood, and had a practice in Sundance as well, delivered you in her office on December 1, 1876.

But, back to when I was a scout. I was in Arizona up to the winter of 1871 and during that time I had a great many adventures with the Indians. I met their scouts and saw their camps and it reminded me of being a child camping outside with my brothers and sisters after our parents were dead. Although I found it easy and best to avoid conflict when called upon, I performed the most dangerous missions. I drew a reputation for getting myself and others safely out of many a close circumstance. I was considered the most daring rider and one of the best shots in the Western country. In truth, after the deaths of Mother, Father, Anne, Silas and Mary, I was reckless because I didn't care if I lived. I had no designs on life. I couldn't even imagine the future. Once or twice I think I set out to get myself killed and then just changed my mind at the last minute. Maybe that's how heroes get made out of men.

After that campaign I returned to Fort Sanders, Wyoming, and remained there until spring of 1872, when we were ordered out to the Mussel Shell Indian Outbreak, sometimes called Nursey Pursey. In that war Generals Custer, Miles, Terry and Crook were all engaged. It was because of something that happened in Goose Creek that I was christened Calamity. Goose Creek is where the town of Sheridan is now. Captain Egan was in command of the post. The Indians were fighting back. I admired them sometimes when they fought us. We were sneaky liars, negotiating in the daytime, and stealing their supplies and horses at night so they would starve and hopefully surrender out of desperation. But on this occasion we were ordered out to quell an uprising of the Indians, and were there for several days. There were numerous bloody skirmishes during which we started to look foolish to ourselves. Six of the soldiers were killed and several were severely wounded. Often I was a nurse through the evening to the men.

In spite of all my accomplishments the men found it hard to respect me. The soldiers thought because they never saw Indians when I was scouting that I was a bad scout. I saw my job as being primarily a protector to the men I led, leading them away from danger. As a child I had seen a Confederate soldier shoot a Union officer who was his own cousin dead. I had seen grief come from every direction. I thought it no mistake that the Indian campaigns came on the heels of quashing seces-sion. I knew that both sides, the North and the South, were sick with what they had done and somehow that was driving them to do worse; shame is a great engine and the Indian wars were partly that engine running on leftover madness from the Civil War. I refused to lead anyone towards that madness.

One night while returning to the post we were ambushed. We were riding too far apart but we were only a mile and a half from safety. I heard some shots and I looked back at Captain Egan behind me. He reeled in his saddle and began to slip from his horse. I turned my horse sharp and rode at a gallop to him. I put my full self into getting there in time to catch him and yank him onto the front of my horse. I caught him still falling and he was bigger than me so the weight practi-cally pulled me down as well. But I lifted him onto my horse and let him lie like a blanket in front of me. It must have hurt him to be in that position as we raced to the fort. But the oth-ers died or got hurt so bad they had to quit for home. I was fine and Captain Egan, on recovering, thanked me and said, I name you Calamity Jane, the Heroine of the Plains. It was a joke. He was grateful but he never thought that highly of me and he never meant to rename me. But I have borne that name up to the present time.

At the end of that campaign we were ordered to Fort Custer, where Custer City now stands. We arrived there in the spring of 1874. It was sunny but cold at night. Mist in the mornings made it so the world was wiped away and then gradually reappeared. The flowers were out in full force; at times it was as if the horses were swimming the blossoms were so high and plentiful. The Black Hills were beautiful, the way they folded into each other. There were happy animals everywhere and birds in the sky. I listened to the turkey vultures, nuthatches and even the frogs as if they were singing for me. I watched the lovely beavers playing by slapping their tails. I talked to the sunflowers, which were tall as me, and I ate the violets. I felt something about South Dakota that felt so sweet and good it almost hurt.

We remained around Fort Custer all summer until we were ordered back to Wyoming, to Fort Russell near Cheyenne, in fall of 1874. We remained there until spring of 1875 and then we were ordered (happily) back to the Black Hills to protect miners from the Sioux. That country had been controlled by the Lakota Sioux since they had defeated the Cheyenne in 1776. The Hills were sacred land and were supposed to be covered by the Laramie Treaty. But Custer's expedition there found gold and nothing could keep the white man out once that news spread. The gold rush brought the army in. We shouldn't have been there, even by our own laws. The Indians got even madder as they realized that the army, which was supposed to be keeping outsiders out, was fighting to protect the miners and settlers. So this turned into a war that some whispered was sparked on purpose by Ulysses S. Grant because he hoped the gold would cure his personal depression. No one denied that the country's depression, which had lasted three years, scared everyone inside and outside of the army.

So that's what happened. You might have heard about different battles: the Battle of Little Bighorn, the Dull Knife Fight, the Battle of Slim Buttes; it all comes down to us telling them to stay on a space of land and then finding something we wanted there and telling them to get off of it. What were they to do? Bighorn was one for them; Dull Knife and Slim Buttes were two for the army. Both sides took terrible losses. No matter who was winning, the soldiers were getting thin and impatient. A lot of soldiers traded bullets for mining equipment and just yelled bang, pretended to die, and disguised themselves to start anew. Eventually both sides gave in to another treaty and the boomtowns became part of the United States of America. I remember walking in Deadwood after that treaty with the strange feeling that all the criminals around me had suddenly been knighted.

In spring of 1876, we were ordered north with General Crook to join the Generals Miles, Terry and Custer at Little Bighorn River. I was the bearer of important dispatches and as the most reckless I was given the job of swimming the Platte River at Fort Fetterman, riding ninety miles to bring news back and forth. I was so wet and cold for so long that I woke up every morning thinking I was dead. I contracted a severe illness and was sent back in General Crook's ambulance to Fort Fetterman, where I lay in the hospital thinking of my family for fourteen days.

As soon as the army didn't need me as a soldier my sex became visible and I was suddenly too frail for duty. I didn't mind. I was ready to have a turn at independence. During the month of April I acted as a Pony Express rider carrying the U.S. mail between Deadwood and Custer, a distance of fifty miles, over one of the roughest trails in Black Hills country. I made the round trip every two days, which I defy you to beat on a fresh horse with no packages.

Many riders before me had been held up and robbed of their packages. But I was too fast, too good a shot, and too famous for anyone to try robbing me. I carried mail and money (for that was the only way of getting mail and money between those points). Once in a while the craftier or stupider toll-gatherers tried to muscle me but mostly I was looked on as a good fellow who never missed his mark.

I always hoped to rejoin the army but instead I met James Butler Hickock, better known as Wild Bill, and we started for Deadwood together, arriving as friends and lovers in about June. I don't know how to speak of love but I hope you find it, Daughter.

I remained around Deadwood all that summer, visiting the camps within an area of one hundred miles. I tried my hand at gold-panning but never saw a flake. I rode around the Plains with Wild Bill, my darling friend, and we remained in Deadwood during the summer. On the second of August 1876, sitting at a gambling table in the Bella Union in Deadwood, he was shot in the back of the head by the notorious desperado Jack McCall. I started to look for the assassin at once and found him at Shurdy's butcher shop. I grabbed a meat cleaver and made him throw up his hands. I had pictures in my head of me killing him, of a surprised look on his face as it fell apart under my blade. Truth is, in all my life I never killed a single person. I was a hunter, but not of human beings. If you want to know the complete truth I could hit a tiny moving target as small as a bee searching in the air for flowers. After my brother and sisters died I aimed at rabbits and deer and even horses and men and I knew I had them perfectly dead beneath my sights but I never squeezed my gun's trigger except for contests and then only at spinning wheels and other foolishness. It wasn't that I thought life was precious. I knew that it wasn't. It was life—cheap and dirty— but life, still.

I cornered Jack McCall, and I frightened him until he saw that I was crying. You cannot dance around with a cleaver in your hand for as long as you would think and still be taken seriously. He was taken to a log cabin and locked up, well secured as everyone thought, but he got away. Afterwards he was caught at Fagan's ranch on Horse Creek, on the Old Cheyenne road, and was then taken to Yankton, where he was tried, sentenced and hung.

Poker Alice comforted me for hours. We were a strange couple to any who saw us: me a weeping mess in pants, and her a solid shoulder and a soft voice saying, Hey, hey, it's going to be all right.

I remained around Deadwood locating claims, going from camp to camp, until the spring of 1877, when one morning, I saddled my horse and rode towards Crook City. I had gone about twelve miles from Deadwood, at the mouth of Whitewood Creek, when I met the overland mail running from Cheyenne to Deadwood. The horses were on a run, about two hundred yards from the station. Upon looking closely I saw that they were pursued by road agents. The horses ran to the barn as was their custom. As the horses stopped I rode alongside of the coach and found the driver, John Slaughter, lying face downwards in the boot of the stage, he having been shot. When the stage got to the station the road agents hid in the bushes. I immediately removed all baggage from the coach except the mail. I then took the driver's seat and with all haste drove to Deadwood, carrying the six passengers and the dead driver to a safe ending.

I left Deadwood in the fall of 1877 and went to Bear Butte Creek with the 7th Cavalry. During the fall and winter we built Fort Meade and the town of Sturgis. In 1878 I left the command and went to Rapid City to spend the year prospecting. The gold still was not interested in me, and so I bullwhacked for a bit.

In 1879 I went to Fort Pierre and drove trains to and from Rapid City for Frank Witch then drove teams from Fort Pierce to Sturgis for Fred Evans. This teaming was done with oxen; even though they were slow they were better fitted for the work than horses, owing to the rough nature of the country.

Over the next few years I drifted: Wyoming, California, Texas, Arizona. I stopped at all points of interest until I reached El Paso in the fall of 1885. While in El Paso, I met Mr. Clinton Burke, a native of Texas, who I married. I had traveled through life long enough alone and it was time to take a partner. We remained in Texas and I began a quiet home life which I meant to last forever.

On October 28th, 1887, I became the mother of a boy baby, the very image of its father, at least that is what he said, but who had the temper of its mother. He lived a few days and I nursed him. I thought of you and how far away I had sent you. I thought maybe I could bring you back. But then he died of the crib death. I held him after the doctor came. I rocked him in the chair we bought for the purpose. I thought how quiet he was and how you had screamed at me as if you knew I was going to be a bad mother from the moment you were born. You were right. You knew everything.

When we left Texas we went to Boulder, where we kept a hotel until 1893. We hosted Belle Starr there and that's how she became my friend. I heard that she was a horse thief and that she helped the James brothers after they robbed the railroad. I thought the law was really after her because she was married to an Indian. She helped me write this for you so take that into consideration.

My husband and I adopted a girl named Marie. She was fat and joyful; she clapped and spoke in baby babble. I loved her and I thought often of you. But I could not quit drinking and my husband gave her away. I cried for twenty days after which I went back where I belonged, traveling on alone through Wyoming, Montana, Idaho, Washington, Oregon, then back to Montana, then to Dakota, arriving in Deadwood on October 9th, 1895, after an absence of seventeen years.

My arrival in Deadwood after such an absence created quite an excitement among my many friends of the past, to such an extent that it spread to a vast number of the citizens who had come to Deadwood during my absence and who had heard of Calamity Jane and her many adventures. Among the many whom I met were several gentlemen from eastern cities who advised me to appear in exhibitions so that people out East would get to see the Famous Woman Scout from the Black Hills.

For a while a woman put me up and she said I could be comfortable to the end of my days. She found me by the river in Deadwood living with Annette, who everyone called Old Nett. She was rude to Nett as many white folks are to coloreds, not knowing or seeing that Nett was my friend who fed me and talked to me and didn't need any stories of the Old West or any shooting displays from me. I followed that rich woman, stumbling out of the mud, to a life I had never known with regular bedding and no worries. All I had to do was stay sober and tell people about my life and shoot a little bit. I was a fool to leave the river. Nett said to me when I was going, You be good, take care of yourself. That was the last I heard of her tender voice. Oh, how I still miss Nett. How we sat at night in silence by the fire and breathed in the woodsmoke. Nett had three children die at birth and three more killed by sickness, accident and murder. We understood each other, how much each of us had lost.

The rich woman arranged for a man named Cummins, who was director of the Indian Congress, to solicit my talents for a traveling show. Cummins had assembled performers from thirty-one tribes for the Trans-Mississippi Exposition and the Omaha Greater American Exhibition. Now everyone was excited about the Pan-American Exposition and it was for that he wanted me. Geronimo would receive top billing, which made me happy because it meant less attention on me. Cummins chartered a trolley car to take me and some of the other performers to the exposition. We stopped at Niagara Falls. I got out and stood at the edge watching tons of frothing water fall over the precipice. The sound was like the biggest mule train stampeding across the Plains. It was a bigger sound than I had ever heard. There was a force behind it like the force that pushes the avalanche down a mountain, or the force in men that starts a war. The fog that poured upwards cooled my skin. I watched my foot on the brink and I closed my eyes. I wanted to let myself fall into that water and be gone. The photographers took pictures of me there. In the newspaper they said I looked as if I could defy the mighty waters.

At the Pan-American Exposition I was like the children. I went on rides: Trip to the Moon, Scenic Railway, Ferris Wheel, Captive Balloon. I watched mock battles in the stadium staged by Buffalo Bill's Wild West show. At first there were so many people to see that I felt awed by the sheer variety of God's work. At sunset I watched the illumination of all the buildings as the thousands of little light bulbs grew bright, and more than once I heard a little girl gasp, Oh, isn't it beautiful? Is it really real?

But then it was up to me and I couldn't do it. I did try to perform myself. My friends bought me a suit worthy of Wild

Bill. But I hated being stared at by strangers. My tongue wouldn't move. I had to drink and so I broke my promise. I got up onstage and all those fancy faces turned towards me expecting me to shine on them. At the back of the auditorium I saw Geronimo watching. That old Apache had a look in his eye that made me want to cry, for although we were not dead, not gone, we were now artifacts of the frontier, which I suddenly realized was utterly gone, never to return. We were stared upon by eyes glistening with the prophecy of our deaths, seeing us as the last animals of extinct species pushed over the edge of the world by the onslaught of money. And we would not be allowed to live much longer.

I felt so sick and so afraid that I puked on the front row and was fired. The rich woman took my pay and Cummins wanted nothing to do with me. I went to see my old friend Buffalo Bill Cody who was there with his Wild West show. He offered me a spot but I said I couldn't do it and he understood. He gave me train fare.

I started home, having just discovered that such a place did not exist for one such as me.

I KNEW then that I was dying and I told the reporters in Deadwood that I came back there for the purpose. Nett was gone from the river. Bill and Charlie were gone. The muddy shantytown that I had loved was built over. The Chinese neighborhood was evacuated. There was no reason left in this world to stay sober. I had helped who I could help and that just never included me. Dora let me work at her place, whatever work I could do, laundry and such. Once in a while someone wanted to pay to lie with a legend and I still had enough tenderness for humanity to agree. I slept poorly under a roof, but I was sad and so I slept as much as I could with all those cats around my head. I wondered, if you ever knew me would you think me a monster or what?

LISTEN, WHEN you grow, if you are a human child and I think you are, you will ask yourself why I gave you up, were you too much to handle or not good enough for me to keep? I expect these will be bitter questions and it hurts me badly to imagine your heart when you think them. Please believe it was all on me. When I looked at you I saw Anne, and Mary, and Silas, and Elijah, and even Lena, and how I couldn't take care of them. You were the mark of a world I could not control.

I saw Bill Hickok with a bullet in his head. I saw my ragged mother and my drunk father and my own shameful self. I knew that if I kept you with me you would die. I would get drunk and leave you to starve or freeze. I would bring home the wrong people. I would gamble away all the money we needed for your shoes and books and dresses. I would get killed one night and leave you helpless. All the risks I'd ever taken flashed through my mind. And looking back at me was this brand-new person who was also the living memory of everyone I had ever loved. You were too precious to stay with me. I saw in you someone who was much too good for me. I guess that every mother looks at her new baby after all that pain, through that shock, and feels that they are seeing some-one amazing, someone they can't possibly deserve. But I was right. I needed more than anything I have ever needed in my life for you to outlive me.

I want you to know that my mother loved me. And my brother Elijah, and my brother Silas, and my sisters, Mary and

Lena and God Almighty's little Anne, they loved me too, but no grown man ever did, not even Bill. Love never made me strong. It never brought out any special reserves in me. I looked at you and all my confidence drained out with the blood between my legs. I could not keep you safe. I could not protect you. Darling girl, I knew that someday somebody might break your heart. But I decided then that it wouldn't be me.

They called me Calamity Jane. They did not call me Slutty Jane or Jane the Drunk or Boy Jane. They called me Calamity. I did not give myself that name and I did not make others use it. I may not be a hero who saved a man on the front of her horse, but to those who say I am not, I say, How do you know that? Was Bill Hickok everything he said? Was he everything that was said about him? Was Jesse James? A hero is someone who does something extraordinary and gets recognized for it. The only reason why I cannot be a hero is that I do extraordinary things all the time. It is expected of me. I cannot leave you any money or any cattle or any land. But I can leave you this, this one thing I know. A lie is a thing. It is a real thing in the world like a diamond or a gold nugget or a name or a hole in the wall. It's real but it only has the meaning you give it. Some think it's valuable, some don't. Some believe in it, some don't. And like a hole in the wall once it's there you can fill it in or cover it up, or elaborate on it, or say that it doesn't affect any other thing, or you can go fuck yourself. The lie doesn't care. Like that hole in the wall it does not care what you do.

I write this so as to tell you who I was or who I am. I write this to speak about MY self in MY words. I write this so that no one can kill me because it seems often that everyone is trying to kill me by forgetting me, ignoring me or giving all the fame to my beloved friends. It's true I never killed anyone, but I nursed dozens back to life. I did things I didn't believe in and others that I am ashamed of. But so did Bill and Buffalo Bill and Charlie. I never betrayed a friend and there were many who loved me regardless of my flaws. I tried to avoid conflict between the white regiments and the Indians. I tried to reject the violence that everyone said was just life; I truly believe that every injury you leave upon another stays with you. And so I tried to injure as few people as possible. And that was more difficult than I can explain.

I would have liked you to meet Poker Alice when she was smoking cigars and cleaning out a table of high-rollers. I'd have liked you to see Annie Oakley and me telling stories on a stage in front of a happy audience. That did happen once or twice. I'd have liked to ask you who you are and hear about it all. But those things can't happen in this lifetime. So I write this hoping that this little history of my life may interest you. I do love you. I love you so much more than I can say.

I remain, alive or dead, forever yours,
Mrs. M. BURKE
Better known as Calamity Jane, Jane Canary, Martha Canary or Your Mother

Miette

|||||||||||||||||||||||||||||||||||||||||||||

I LAID MY FACE ON MY PILLOW FOR AN HOUR AND then I went to Dora. She told me to go to Terry to find her. There had been an incident and she was sick on the ore-train. I borrowed a horse to ride. At the brink of town the wolf was there. It was the most venomous day of summer; all the flowers had gone rotten in the heat and the stench was like the armpit of someone you used to love. The road under our ten feet—the horse's four solid hooves, the wolf's paws and my two dangling flesh mitts—went up and down and seemed to rock like water. It's always downhill at the end. I spoke out loud to myself and pretended I could see my destination.

I expected to find her by her own light, to see her radiating in the dark with all the stories of gambling and drinking and whoring under great skies surrounding her. I was so dazed from her letter and so afraid of her. For no reason I can fathom I remembered something from a story about a gate that led to the only green field and a plain of corn impossible except for the bottomless will of an English farmer. From the other side of that gate, across that field, you can see the Badlands, shining at night because the earth is white, I whispered, telling lies. The earth isn't white in the Badlands, it is red, orange, brown, purple, black, but never white.

We, the wolf, the horse and me, made our way down a steep incline between rock faces. The long echoes of clickety-clop-clip-clop-clickety-clop-clip-clop made it seem as if we were at the head of a train of obedient burrow ghosts, our eyes bulging from the heat that poured off the hard spiky surfaces all around us.

SHE WAS lying on the floor, thin as a woman could be and still be alive. Her mouth was open, gaping as if she were asleep. A tin can sang as it collected one out of every thousand raindrops that fell from the roof.

I stepped inside and shuddered at the smell of shit and vomit, of deathly sickness, dirt and whisky. She looked up and in her gaze was the cannonball coming for me.

Hello, dear, she said. Her voice was thick and hard to understand.

Hello, darlin', I said.

The train conductor left me here, she said and sighed in a frightening way, as if to expel all the air left in her body. I guess I misbehaved.

Her skin was white and powdery. Her eyes were yellow. Her face was so lined and the lips so collapsed she looked ninety. Her eyelids were brown and shriveled about her eyeballs.

How long have you been here? I asked, wondering what sort of man would carry a woman, however drunk, off of a train and leave her in an abandoned cabin alone to die.

She shrugged and a sound of gases welled up from her stomach. She started to cry.

I SLIPPED my arms beneath her and lifted her. I carried my mother like some broken bride-doll back across the threshold to the waiting horse. I flopped her unceremoniously into the saddle and rode them both back into Deadwood. I took her straight to Dora's place because I knew we wouldn't be turned away.

Dora gave us her own room, which was clean and light and filled with chintz and lace curtains and pillows and embroidered blankets and painted furniture. Calamity laughed to see herself in the mirror with all of Heaven reflected behind her. There were mirrors everywhere; the vanity, the bureau was made of mirrors. A full-length three-part mirror stood by the windows, the jewelry box was mirrored, and on the wall hung a large oval mirror in a gilt frame. All these surfaces reflected her back in multiples that suggested a crystal growing. She looked at herself and cocked her head like a puppy and sighed.

I washed her in the tub and saw the scars beneath the bruises, yellow bruises and red bruises and bruises where the blood seeped through, all over her arms and torso. Her breasts were collapsed; her ribs were sculpted out of driftwood. She lay in the warm water with her eyes closed and a hand over her eyes. When she moaned I asked if she felt sick and brought a bucket but there was nothing left inside her. I used Dora's soaps and shampoo and the pink sponge she had in a porcelain dish. I rubbed my mother's arms and scrubbed her fingers and nails and cleaned her back and behind and between until she was rosy from the rubbing. She had no strength left and so I lifted her with my two arms wrapped around her waist. She retched but could not vomit. Her feet hovered above the wet rug shaped like a rosebud. I left my footprints there.

I dried her propped against the wall and walked her to the bed and sat her down wrapped in a warm dry towel. Dora had been standing by and she took the clothes. I apologized but she said nothing, only shook her head. I wrapped my mother in one of Dora's robes, shiny white silk with purple flowers blossoming across the back.

It's soft, she said.

You take a bath, said Dora. I'll watch her. You don't want to get her dirty again.

I bathed as quick as I could. Dora gave me another robe and gathered my clothes with my mother's and left us. The door closed and we were alone together, she lying on the bed and me standing over her.

Dora gave me your letter, I said.

She showed no understanding.

My father sent me to find you.

She opened her eyes and looked at me. We camped, she said.

What?

After Mama died and Daddy died, we camped. The Indians showed us how. We followed the soldiers and stayed outside the forts. Sometimes the soldiers gave us food.

But they didn't take you in?

She shook her head. Only the Indians ever took us in.

I held her head to help her sip water. I tried to give her soup but she was beyond eating. I sat beside the bed and watched her. I held her hand and rubbed her palm. Her breathing was labored and when she coughed it was a painful wet dig for air.

TREMORS TOOK her in the night and I got into the bed to hold her, to keep her from falling apart. I curved my body around hers and held her tightly, her back against my belly, her legs bent and knees to her chest and held there by my arm. I breathed into her hair. Half the time her mouth was so sticky I couldn't understand what she said. She might have been dreaming or she might have been seeing the people to whom she spoke. She spoke to my father and asked him to care for me. She spoke to Charlie and Dora. She spoke to her brother Elijah, begging him not to resurrect her. She spoke to her stepdaughter Jesse. She asked Jesse where she was and then she covered her face and cried. I wanted her to speak to me. I wanted her to look at me and know who I was but I couldn't say that. I couldn't hurt her and break the only minutes we had together.

Once she looked at me with all the warmth and understanding of an old friend. I lay on the floor and rolled back and forth over the aches in my belly, my back and my chest. I crushed my eyes with my fingers. I surrendered the idea of asking her anything. There was nothing left to do but forgive. The woman was dying in my arms and all I could think was how, in fact, I loved her. It was a bone stuck in my throat. Her breathing slowed and she asked for a drink.

Just one drink to toast you? she said.

No, it's better that you don't. Do you want me to sing to you? My father used to like me to sing.

Is he dead?

Yes.

Were you there with your father when he died?

Yes.

Was it terrible? Was it terrible to die?

No. He knew he was going to Heaven.

What about me? she cried. What if you are not going to Heaven?

Are you in pain?

Yes, she cried and then she wept, and I shushed her and rocked her in my arms and held her hands and squeezed them. I rubbed her arms and back and stroked her hair. I weighed her body, light as paper ashes, against mine.

Her bladder and bowels by then were dry and her stomach was concave. I saw her hair fall out when she turned her head on the pillow. I sat in a rocking chair by the window and looked out over Deadwood. The streets were lit and the people walking along the paved roads between the pretty brick Victorian buildings seemed civilized and carefree. I felt as if I watched them from the moon.

A wolf showed me where you were.

I always liked wolves, she said.

Yes, well, it seems like that was clear.

That's good.

I looked at her thinking, if I only get a few questions, what should they be?

Where were you born?

I don't remember. Don't cry. Why are you crying? Your eyes are so light, she said.

My eyes.

Yes, your eyes are so light. I like them.

I like your eyes too, I said.

THE LAST hours of her life passed in silence but we were together. I held her hand and rubbed circles in her motionless palm with my thumb. Dora brought us a phonograph and kept music playing. I looked up at her when she came in but I never could speak. There was a hard nut of pain in my chest. I rubbed at my breast bone and coughed but the pain didn't care. I tried out words that children call their mothers, pushed them around with my tongue while I watched her. I might as well have pulled arrows from my flesh.

I heard a rattle from the bed and when I touched her wrist I knew she was gone. It was gentle as far as death goes. Downstairs the girls were laughing and people were drunk and happy. A tabby cat threaded between my legs and rolled on its back and rubbed its softness on my feet. Kittens mewled in the closet. I heard a car outside, a sound I could not get used to, and the train whistle, farther off, described an elaborating distance. I went to her and kissed her.

Martha and Miette

|||||||||||||||||||||||||||||||||||||||||||||||||

HER CLOTHES WERE SMELLY RAGS SO DORA AND I dressed her in one of Dora's white nightgowns. It was very loose about her but the sleeves were not long enough to cover her wrists. The town paid for a walnut coffin lined with ruffled silver silk. The coffin-maker had the coffin brought to the room. Dora and I lifted her body and let her down into the silk. I smoothed the folds of white cotton around her body and then rearranged them because they revealed too much of her bones. Dora put one of her own books by my mother's hip. I put the Jules Verne book beside her cheek, thinking perhaps she could read it in the afterlife. We tucked her hair into a neat bun. She was stark but we decided not to paint her.

The girls all came into the room to say goodbye. A very young prostitute named Sara held up a kitten to kiss my mother's cheek with its rasping tongue. Joannie put a mirror in beside my mother's hand. Feathers and flowers and cards bearing aces and drawings of hearts and foreign coins all were made to dress her simple uniform.

There was a parade. Men in fine suits and stovepipe hats carried her in her coffin down the main street past the weeping, bleary crowds. A drummer and trumpet player and a little boy carrying Old Glory led the procession. I walked at the back. The Chinese scattered red papers riddled with holes all around the streets.

It will slow the Devil down, Dora whispered. He has to pass through every hole before he can get to her.

Someone threw a book at me and when I caught it I saw that it was a novel about her. Everywhere, people embraced me. They gripped my shoulders and turned me around and looked in my eyes and stroked my face. Their tears fell on my neck and hands. The stories of her good deeds began to harmonize. The sheriff gave a speech over her open grave and looked up to Heaven and held out his arms and thanked God for her. Dora held me up, put her arm about my waist when I staggered. One of Dora's girls stood at the head of the grave. She was dressed in a white gown with a full bustle and a plunging neckline. She held an ivory bone fan that she waved in front of her face as she sang the coffin into the ground.

> Oh can there be in life a charm,
> More sweet that retrospection lends,
> When dwells the heart with rapture warm,
> On past delights and absent friends,
> When dwells the heart with rapture warm,
> On past delights and absent friends.
> That soothing charm I would not lose,
> For all the bliss that wealth attends;
> That soothing charm I would not lose,
> For all the bliss that wealth attends;
> Its joys could ne'er a calm infuse,
> So sweet as thought
> Of Absent friends,

Of Absent friends,
Of Absent friends,
Of Absent friends,
Of Absent friends,
Of Absent friends,
Of Absent friends.

Later that night a production called *Life of Calamity* was improvised upon the stage at the Bella Union. I sat in the front row of the darkened auditorium sipping wine, long-stemmed roses on my lap. Dora, seated beside me, held my free hand. A voice began to sing *a cappella* and it was as if that voice created a space so that it could be joined by another and another and another as the lights rose to show the cast. Calamity Jane lay in the arms of her long-lost daughter; Wild Bill embraced his wife Agnes with Charlie Utter looking on; Lew Spencer laughed as he stood arm in arm with the Queen of the Blondes and her two blonde companions. In the background, a line of people moved through a series of tableaux, staging scenes about work, of panning for gold, of farming, of tending to the sick and to the lonely, of providing entertainment and sex, of cooking and doing laundry, of digging graves and saying goodbye.

Epilogue for Imogen

|||||||||||||||||||||||||||||||||||||||||||||||||

WHAT ARE WE TO DO WITH THIS, MY SWEET AND wonderful girl? What should be written on the tombstones of legends? Wild Bill is buried on a hill beneath a bronze bust of himself looking young and formal. The epitaph, written by Charlie Utter, reads, *Pard, we will meet again in the Happy Hunting Ground. To part no more, goodbye.*

Buffalo Bill is buried at Lookout Mountain overlooking the Great Plains and the mountains, the Continental Divide, the ponderosa pines. His tombstone is fashioned out of blond rocks cemented together in the shape of a chimney. A plaque gives his name and the dates of his birth and his death and says that he was a *Noted Scout and Indian Fighter.*

Crowfoot is buried with his horse. He was dressed in a buckskin suit with a feather headpiece adorned with a stuffed crow and solemnly carried with his saddle and rifle to a burial place on a rise overlooking Blackfoot Crossing, where Treaty 7 was signed. A bronze marker on the grave reads that he was *Father of His People.* In 1948 a stone cairn was also erected there in his honor.

Sitting Bull was buried in Post Cemetery, of Fort Yates, North Dakota. His gravestone is a tall marble pedestal supporting a three-ton granite bust of him on an elevated shrine with a flagpole that flies the American flag. His epitaph reads, *Chief of the Hunkpapa Sioux.*

Jesse James is buried by his wife and cousin Zerelda under a stone that stands for both of them and gives the dates of their beginnings and endings, commenting only that he was assassinated.

Belle Starr, the Bandit Queen, is buried on her ranch. Her stone bears a poem by her proud daughter Pearl:

Shed not for her the bitter tear,
Nor give the heart to vain regret;
'Tis but the casket that lies here,
The gem that filled it sparkles yet.

Doubt hangs about the contents of some of these graves and that of Red Cloud, and Geronimo. But no one imagines that Calamity Jane is not where she belongs. Dead on August 1st, 1903, buried on August 6th. Stories of who had stood by her deathbed—who had warned her of her death, who knew her, who had loved her, been loved by her—blossomed over her grand funeral.

She is buried in a modest grave in Mount Moriah Cemetery beside Bill Hickok and all the poor whose gravestones make up Potter's Field. Two-thirds of 3,600 graves in Mount Moriah are paupers' graves marked this way. Martha's grave shows that her alias was Calamity Jane and that she requested to be buried by Bill. There was some confusion when the headstone was carved and it reads that she died on August 2nd, the anniversary of Wild Bill's murder. This is an error no one bothers to correct, what with the value of stone. These are the stories of your ancestors. I give them to you because my grandmother and my mother loved me and I love you. One day I hope you will know how when you love a daughter it breaks the spine of history and folds time all around you. After horses there were carriages then cars then Bennett buggies and subways and then, who knows? There may be other cousins out there roaming about that you could meet someday, children of children of children had by Burke or by Steer's daughter, Jesse, or by her other husbands, little lives that went unrecorded. If they exist I hope you find one another.

I love you and your brother so very, very much.

A Note on Pastiche Sources

||||||||||||||||||||||||||||||||||||||||||||||||||||

THIS NOVEL IS A WORK OF METAHISTORIOGRAPHIC fiction. Most of the facts about Calamity Jane, including who she was at birth, are difficult to prove. The woman named Martha Canary (sometimes Cannary or Burke), who became famous as Calamity Jane, claimed to have had a daughter by Wild Bill Hickok that she gave up for adoption, and it is out of this claim that the story of Miette was born. The novel and its arrangement are original, but almost every character—with the significant exceptions of the protagonist, her father, Zita and the Hag—is a real historical figure and wherever possible I use their words and their descriptions of the events that they were part of. In the sections where direct quoting at length occurs, the original, historical document has been altered to allow the novel to transition smoothly from scene to scene and to make these voices better aid the overall project. However, it is worth noting the sources of sections where real voices and other texts appear. The list that follows does not include the apocryphal quotes (the quote by Lincoln upon meeting Harriet Beecher Stowe, for example) or any other facts or stories drawn from secondary descriptions of conversations, or events drawn from nonfiction sources that are not first-person accounts.

Juan Rulfo's classic magic realist novel *Pedro Páramo* influenced the early chapters of the book. In fact, at one time I saw Miette's story as a contemporary revisiting of his novel, which is the story of a man sent on a journey by his dying sainted mother to find his infamous criminal father.

Text from Jules Verne's novel *Five Weeks in a Balloon* was adapted (where I preferred my own French) from a translation made available by Project Gutenberg. The text I adapted can be viewed here: www.gutenberg.org/ebooks/3526.

The text of the pamphlet handed out by Maguire describing Calamity Jane is from James D. McLaird's critical biography *Calamity Jane*.

Theophilus Little's account is drawn from a description of his life in Abilene written in a loose-leaf notebook. It is altered via editing and rewrites to highlight Wild Bill Hickok's story. It can be viewed here: www.rootsweb.ancestry.com/~pasulliv/settlers/settlers25/WildBill.htm.

Lew Spencer's long speech is drawn in part from the memoir of another "Negro minstrel" named Ralph Keeler. That speech is rewritten and fictionalized to reflect the information I had about Lew, to better fit the novel and to conjure greater connection between Lew and Calamity Jane. The original (fascinating) Ralph Keeler story can be viewed here: www.circushistory.org/Cork/BurntCork5.htm#KEELER.

The description of Calamity Jane attributed to Charlie Utter is a highly contentious bit of text that may or may not have been invented by one biographer and then plagiarized by several others. It can be viewed here: www.deadwoodmagazine. com/archivedsite/Archives/Girls_Calamity.htm.

THE ARTICLE by Lavinia Hart has been edited for length. The complete article can be read here: panam1901.org/ documents/dochumannature.html.

CALAMITY JANE's letter to Miette is based on Calamity Jane's autobiography, a pamphlet she sold on the street close to the end of her life to make a small amount of money. It has been greatly expanded in my version and recast as something not meant for public circulation. The original pamphlet can be viewed here: www.worldwideschool.org/library/books/hst/biography/ LifeAdventuresCalamityJane/Chap1.html.

BLACKFOOT STORIES and beliefs appear in parts of Zita's speeches. A great resource for Blackfoot culture is the beautiful and amazing Blackfoot Crossing Historical Centre in Alberta. I highly recommend a visit: www.blackfootcrossing.ca.

THE SONG lyrics are from songs that were popular in America in the nineteenth century. They would have been in circulation throughout Calamity Jane's lifetime. They can be viewed here: pdmusic.org/1800s.html.

Acknowledgements

||||||||||||||||||||||||||||||||||||||||||||||||||

THIS BOOK HAD MANY TIRELESS CHAMPIONS FOR whom I am utterly grateful. Thank you, Hilary McMahon, for finding us a wonderful home. Thank you to my passionate editors Lea Beresford at Bloomsbury and Jennifer Lambert and Jane Warren at HarperCollins for pushing me forward with your uncompromising vision. Thank you to Patrick Crean for your support, advice and guidance through the first years of this project. Thank you, Susan Swan, for your constant support, your friendship and your mentoring.

Thank you to Tom Wayman and Suzette Mayr, whose talent and commitment made this book (and my PhD in general) possible. Thank you also to the members of my committee for your thoughtful interrogations, your keen insights and your experience: Mary Polito, Rod McGillis, Elizabeth Jameson, Cecily Deveraux.

Thank you to the support staff in the University of Calgary Department of English, especially Barb Howe. Thank you to Russell Caple, Tasha Hubbard, Jonathan Ball, Nikki Sheppy, Ryan Fitzpatrick, Dennis Vanderspek, Michelle Berry, Angie Abdou and Suzanne Caple-Hicks for your feedback and advice as I worked on the novel and/or on the exegesis. Thank you, Colin Martin, for delivering my dissertation when I was far away.

Thank you, thank you, thank you, and I love you, to my husband and best friend Jeremy Leipert. Thank you to my adored family, especially my mother, Patricia Caple. I hope I make you proud. Thank you to my ideal in-laws. Thank you to my children, Cassius and Imogen Leipert, for keeping me from sliding off the world into the chaos of my imagination. Thank you (always) old friend, Nick Kazamia.

I am very grateful for the financial support of the Alberta Foundation for the Arts, the Department of English and the University of Calgary, a Ralph Steinhauer Award of Distinction, a Ruby University Anniversary Award, several Queen Elizabeth the Second awards and the A.T.J. Cairns Memorial Graduate Scholarship.

A Note on the Author

NATALEE CAPLE is the author of six previous books of internationally acclaimed fiction and poetry, including the novel *Mackerel Sky* and the story collection *The Heart is Its Own Reason*. Her collection of poetry, *A More Tender Ocean*, was shortlisted for the Gerald Lampert Memorial Award. Natalee's work has been nominated for a National Magazine Award, the Journey Prize, the RBC Bronwen Wallace Award, and the Eden Mills Short Fiction Prize. She holds a Ph.D. in English from the University of Calgary, and works as a professor of English literature and creative writing at Brock University. She lives in Ontario, Canada.